ABDUCTION of a SLAVE

The Kate Shugak series

A Cold Day for Murder
A Fatal Thaw
Dead in the Water
A Cold Blooded Business
Play with Fire
Blood Will Tell
Breakup
Killing Grounds
Hunter's Moon
Midnight Come Again
The Singing of the Dead
A Fine and Bitter Snow
A Grave Denied
A Taint in the Blood
A Deeper Sleep
Whisper to the Blood
A Night Too Dark
Though Not Dead
Restless in the Grave
Bad Blood
Less Than a Treason
No Fixed Line
Not the Ones Dead

The Liam Campbell series

Fire and Ice
So Sure of Death
Nothing Gold Can Stay
Better to Rest
Spoils of the Dead

✳

The Eye of Isis series

Death of an Eye
Disappearance of a Scribe
Theft of an Idol

✳

Blindfold Game
Prepared for Rage
Silk and Song
The Collected Short
Stories and Essays
Alaska Traveler
On Patrol With the US
Coast Guard

DANA STABENOW

ABDUCTION *of a* SLAVE

An Aries Book

9 7 5 3 1 2 4 6 8

A catalogue record for this book is available from the British Library.

ISBN (HB): 9781035910069
ISBN (E): 9781035910052

Cover design: Matt Bray | Head of Zeus

Printed and bound in Great Britain by
CPI Group (UK) Ltd, Croydon CR0 4YY

MIX
Paper | Supporting
responsible forestry
FSC   FSC® C171272
www.fsc.org

Head of Zeus Ltd
First Floor East
5–8 Hardwick Street
London EC1R 4RG

WWW.HEADOFZEUS.COM

for the C/Katherines the Great

Cornelia Metella would fit right in

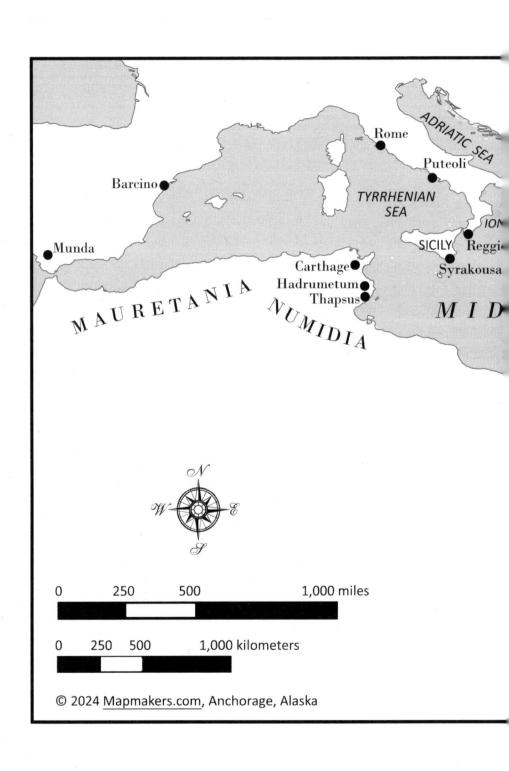

Rome

ADRIATIC SEA

Puteoli

Barcino

TYRRHENIAN
SEA

ION

Munda

SICILY Reggi

Carthage

Syrakousa

Hadrumetum

Thapsus

M I D

M A U R E T A N I A

N U M I D I A

N
W   E
S

0   250   500   1,000 miles

0   250   500   1,000 kilometers

© 2024 Mapmakers.com, Anchorage, Alaska

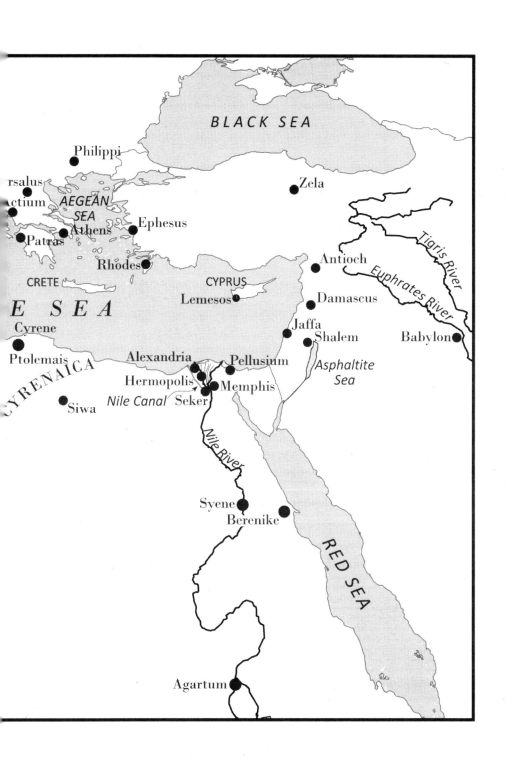

CAST OF CHARACTERS

Acacius	A builder of Alexandria
Apollodorus	Partner in the Five Soldiers
Aristander	Head of the Shurta, the Alexandrian police (wife Merti)
Arsinoë	Cleopatra VII's sister
Aurelius Cotta	Roman legate to Alexandria and Egypt, Julius Caesar's cousin
Babak	Head of the Order of the Owl (in company with Roshanak, Agape, Narses, Bradan)
Bocchus II	King of Mauretania
Caesarion	Son of Cleopatra VII and Julius Caesar
Calliope	A hetaira of Alexandria
Calvin	A customs agent in Cyrene, with Tullus
Castus	Partner in the Five Soldiers
Charmion	Cleopatra's personal servant and administrative aide
Cleopatra VII	Queen of Alexandria and Egypt
Cornelia Metella	Pompey the Great's widow, sister of Metellus Scipio

Crixus	Partner in the Five Soldiers
Demetrius	A builder of ships of Alexandria
Dubnorix	Partner in the Five Soldiers
Elphis	A slave in the house of Laurus
Fulvio	Aurelius Cotta's manservant
Horemheb	Secretary to Cleopatra
Iras	Cleopatra's personal servant and head housekeeper
Isidorus	Partner in the Five Soldiers
Jerome	Captain of the *Hapi II*
Juba I	King of Cyrenaica
Judoc	Spice merchant of Alexandria
Julius Caesar	General, Senator and Consul of Rome
Keren	A physician and a member of House Nebenteru in Alexandria
Laurus	An arms merchant of Cyrene
Markos	Captain of the *Nut*
Metellus Scipio	Supporter of Pompey, ally of Juba, brother to Cornelia
Nebenteru	Tetisheri's uncle and partner in Sea to Sea Imports
Nebet	A cook in Nebenteru's household
Nike	A member of Nebenteru's household
Pastor	Optio in the Roman Army, retired
Phoebe	Cook for Uncle Neb's household
Phryne	Calliope's steward
Ptolemy XII	Cleopatra's father (Auletes)
Ptolemy XIII	Cleopatra's brother, deceased (Theo)
Ptolemy XIV	Cleopatra's brother, husband, and co-ruler (Philo)

Ptolemy XV	Cleopatra's son by Julius Caesar (see Caesarion)
Rhode	Cabria to House Nebenteru
Sextus Pompey	Son of Pompey the Great, stepson of Cornelia Metella
Sosigenes	Chief Librarian of the Great Library, advisor to Queen Cleopatra
Tetisheri	Nebenteru's partner and niece, the 28th Eye of Isis
Timur	Cyrene factor for Nebenteru
Titrit	Cook in the House of Laurus
Tullus	A customs agent in Cyrene, with Calvin
Urania	A slave in the house of Laurus
Vitruvius	Roman engineer and architect

PRÓLOGOS

I t was a beautiful morning, a sky as blue as the sea, a soft breeze keeping the biting flies off. She laid another bunch of dark, red grapes gently in the basket at her feet. She ate one and felt the small, sweet burst of flavor fill her mouth, always with that aftertaste of tartness that gave her village's wine its reputation.

She stood up, seeing the stooping figures of the rest of the girls filling their own baskets. Her best friend, Sophronia, winked at her and she grinned back.

"Ranny!"

Ranny looked up to see Pipi waving from the edge of the vineyard, where the grapes grew closest to the edge of the cliff. She shook her head and bent over to pick up her basket.

"No! Leave it! Come see, Ranny! Now!"

She looked up sharply at the urgency she heard in her

little sister's voice. She left the basket, full of grapes warm from the sun, hiked up her tunic and set off up the path between the vines at a trot. She arrived at her sister's side and followed the pointing finger with her gaze.

Her heart gave a single bound in her breast and then seemed to stop beating altogether.

A ship with a faded sail and steadily beating oars was taking advantage of a combination of the incoming tide and an onshore breeze. Its sides were lined with men in mismatched apparel armed with swords and clubs.

Pipi looked from the ship to her older sister, her expression fearful. "Ranny?"

Ranny tore her eyes from the sea to her sister and bent over, grasping her sister's shoulders tightly in her hands. "Run, Pipi! Run as fast as ever you can to the fields! Tell the men to come at once! Tell them—tell them pirates have come into the cove!"

She stood up and turned her sister around and gave her a shove. Pipi stumbled a few steps and turned to look up at her. "But—what about Mother? And Auntie? And Grandmother? And the babies?"

"I'll warn them! Go!" She gave Pipi another shove, harder this time, so that she nearly fell. "RUN!"

Pipi turned and ran as only a terrified child can, plowing straight through the lines of vines. Ranny watched long enough to see her vanish over the ridge before she turned. "Sophy! Sophronia!"

The other girl stood, shading her eyes in Ranny's direction.

"Pirates!"

Sophronia cocked her head.

"Pirates!" She gave a broad sweep of her arm in the direction of the barley fields. "PIRATES! RUN!"

Without waiting to see if she'd been understood she turned and began to run herself, down the hill, leaping strides, stumbling but not daring to fall, her arms and legs scratched and bleeding first from the vines and then from scrub brush. She shrieked at the top of her voice as she ran, as much as the increasing shortness of breath and the growing stitch in her side would allow. "Pirates! Pirates! Run, run, run! Pirates! Mother! Auntie! PIRATES! RUN!"

The other girls passed her in the other direction with terrified expressions on their faces, baskets of spilled grapes abandoned behind them. Then she was in the olive grove on the north side of the village. Through the shining green leaves she could catch glimpses of the sail, once red and now bleached by the sun to a pale brown. It was the shade of the graceful bowls her mother and her auntie made from the clay deposits near the village and sold at the weekly market to buyers from as far away as the storied cities of Smyrna and Ephesus. It was the color of the sail that enraged her more than anything else; that pirates, thieves, animals who lived only to prey upon others should appropriate that color for themselves. She wanted to stop them in their blasphemy. She wanted to hit them, stab them, hurt them. She wanted to kill them.

But it was already too late when she crashed through the last stand of acacia, to find the bow of the ship run up on the edge of the shingle and men leaping down into the water and wading ashore. Women were snatching up children and running as fast as they could in every direction. Some few escaped but most were caught by the pirates and held in a ragged circle under guard. The air was filled with screaming and crying. Doors were kicked in and sacks of grain and barley and broad beans were carried out. Amphoras full of wine and olive oil followed, and then they discovered the treasure trove of the pottery.

She saw her mother, babies in arms, fleeing toward the hill, caught just before the line of trees. The babies were torn from her arms and she launched herself after them, shrieking. A clenched fist caught her on the cheek and knocked her to the ground, senseless. The same fist yanked up her tunic and its owner fell on her, forcing her legs apart and braying his brute satisfaction to the same blue sky that had seemed so gentle and peaceful not half an hour before.

Grandmother lay in front of the pottery, gray head at a twisted angle, eyes staring sightlessly, hands that had held generations of art and craft in them open, empty, useless now.

The anger drained out of Ranny, leaving her empty of anything but fear. There was nothing she could do here. She turned to run.

Too late, again. A rough hand closed hard over her elbow. "What's this? Running from the nice man?" An unshaven face thrust itself into hers. It belonged to an enormous hulk of a man, balding, scarred over every inch of skin exposed by a short sleeveless tunic. One scar, still deep and red and angry, puckered the skin of his arm from wrist to elbow. In her fear she focused on it rather than on his face, but she couldn't stop her ears. "Hah! Pretty little thing, aren't you? Too young, but you'll soon grow out of that. And there's plenty in the markets who will pay a high price for young, anyway."

He turned toward the ship, pulling her after him. She fought, scratching, kicking, biting, hatred replacing the fear. Not a moment a slave, and the loathing of the captive for the captor was already strong in her.

She found herself raised up off the ground, legs kicking uselessly out of reach. His Greek was rough and ungrammatical but understandable. "Now, now, none of that, girl. I might have to hurt you and we can't be damaging the merchandise, now can we?"

They reached the shore. He waded into the water without hesitation and tossed her up over the side into waiting hands.

She twisted in those hands for a last sight of her village. Laughing men passed women and children and jars and sacks and bleating goats hand to hand from shore to ship. Torches ignited the roofs of houses, here her own, there the headman's, over there the little Temple of Hera where the priestess led them in prayer.

There was no sign of the goddess today.

When the sail was raised again, the only movement she could see on shore was that of the black smoke from the burning buildings, carrying the village and all its memories up into the sky.

1

NOVEMBER 30, 47 BCE
ALEXANDRIA

There was a loud bang from overhead, followed by a panicked cry, some excited shouts, a thump, a bump, and a frantic scrabble of many hands and feet. Tetisheri, sitting in Uncle Neb's office, looked up from a mound of paperwork to see a foot and a hand dangling outside the window. Both were rapidly withdrawn. In their place appeared an upside-down head, which gave voice. "Sorry about that, Neb."

From the other side of his desk Uncle Neb rubbed his eyes. "Anyone hurt?"

The head grimaced. "Not for lack of trying. If that fool Darib weren't a genius at laying tile I'd have let him fall right into the open jaws of his precious Anubis."

"All well then."

"All well, Neb."

"How much longer, Acacius?" Tetisheri tried and failed not to sound as long-suffering as she felt.

The upside-down head grinned at her. "A few days more, lady."

"You said that yesterday."

"I did, didn't I?" Acacius spoke with all the cheerfulness of a builder who knows the current project is too far along for him to be dismissed.

"You are a rogue and a swindler, Acacius."

The upside-down head managed to effect the semblance of a gratified bow. "You are as perspicacious as you are beautiful, lady."

She sighed. "Phoebe told me to tell you that she has something special in store for your lot this evening. Don't be late."

"To be late for one of Phoebe's meals would be an affront to Dionysus himself. Pray tell her we shall not fail of a timely arrival."

Tetisheri said, she thought craftily, "And for how many more days should Phoebe keep the kitchen in readiness for such arrivals?"

The upside-down face assumed the expression of one taking a vow. "A few days more, lady."

Nebenteru started to laugh, caught Tetisheri's eye, and thought better of it. He waved a dismissive hand and the upside-down head retreated rapidly upwards. It was better scene-shifting than Ninos could manage for a play at the Odeum.

"You encourage him, Uncle." But it was said without heat.

Neb gave her a guilty smile. "He amuses me. And he has done some splendid work on the remodel."

"He has that." She sat back with a sigh and massaged her lower back.

She had been home for over a month, after having been absent from Alexandria for longer than that, first on business of the queen, and ending with a voyage upriver to Syene and a much longer journey down. She felt a flush creep up into her cheeks as she recalled certain events along the way. It had been a most memorable trip.

The plans to remodel House Nebenteru had been in the works for a while and Uncle Neb had waited only upon her absence to put them into effect. She had returned to a hollowed out shell where her home had once stood, with Phoebe and Nebet cooking over an open fire in the back garden. Carpenters and masons and plumbers and pipelayers and tilers deafened everyone with their hammers and saws and their oaths and the air was filled with a fine dust that had everyone sneezing from morn till night. She had accused Neb of emptying out Rhakotis, and he didn't deny it. She wondered what the queen was doing for builders in the meantime, and thought on the whole it was best not to inquire.

Neb had purchased the warehouses on either side of the existing house and warehouse and hired an architect friend to draw up plans to assemble all three into one building, comprising the office, warehouse, and residence of what Neb had renamed—in what Tetisheri could only imagine a fit of romantic fervor—Middle Sea Merchant Adventurers. She managed to talk him down to the more staid and more accurate Sea to Sea Imports, although he did have a tendency to pout whenever he was reminded of the change. But as Tetisheri pointed out, at least they didn't have to change the livery of staff and employees, who could still be recognized by the badge of the striped sail.

Uncle Neb wasn't wrong about the growing population of their household, though, especially since Apollodorus had joined it. With Uncle Neb, Tetisheri, Keren, Nike, Phoebe, Nebet, Babak and the other four Owls, Rhode, their new house cabria, plus assorted maids, just one gardener, and Bast, the living god to House Nebenteru, their home had begun to feel a trifle cramped.

Not that Apollodorus was currently in residence, because Her High and Mightiness had sent him away on yet another mysterious mission the instant he and Tetisheri had returned to Alexandria. Something to do with whatever Julius Caesar was up to after annihilating Pontus, was Tetisheri's guess. The latest news had Caesar back in Rome putting out all the fires his enemies had set while he'd been away and for the most part succeeding. Too many of Pompey's family and supporters had escaped Caesar's clutches for him to rest easy in Rome for long, however, and she fully expected to hear before long that he was back under arms somewhere around the Middle Sea. Rumor had it some of the Pompeiians had fled to Cyrenaica. Its king, Juba I, was no friend of Caesar's.

Meanwhile, in Alexandria, Phokas, the architect, had done a good job with the redesign of the house, as even Tetisheri, in spite of being allowed no say in them, had to admit. The business entrance faced Hermes Street at the east end of the new building. The residence took up the center and west end, with a separate entrance and a new atrium created around a large square with columns in the ancient Greek style and a new fountain. The fountain contained a central plinth supporting three statues, one of Hermes, one of Mercury, and one of Hathor. So did Neb cover all his bets in entreating the blessings of the gods who watched over trade in the Middle Sea. When she first saw it Tetisheri made a mental note not to invite any priests of any sect home for dinner.

The back of the new building was dedicated to the warehouse facing the docks and the Port of Eunostos, and was presided over by its own statue, that of Hapi, god of the Nile, which was painted a brilliant blue and green. It was fast becoming a place for Egyptian sailors to pray for fair winds and a following sea—and no pirates—before setting sail. The remodel had doubled the size of the warehouse, improved the docks and created a new and larger strongroom where the luxury goods were secured. The key to the brand new lock, both forged from the same steel as a Roman gladius, was the size and weight of a fireplace poker and was itself kept under lock and its own key.

The warehouse and the docks were what made everything else possible, and Phokas had accorded them the respect they deserved. That he knew they were also the source of his fee was undoubtedly a motivator.

The stables were now enclosed and the quarters above them connected to the rest of the house. The ceilings were higher with windows across the top of every outside wall, which made for a considerable and welcome lowering of the interior temperature during warmer days. There were more spacious private rooms, and the public rooms would do a nomarch proud.

Tetisheri, remembering the queen's tendency to assimilate any Alexandrian structure she took a fancy to into the Royal Palace properties, was of two minds about inviting her to dinner any time soon, either.

The plasterers and the painters had done the exterior first, had finished the private rooms next and were now working on the public rooms. The roof, three times its former size and of different levels, was providing its own problems but, despite the previous conversation, Neb and Tetisheri knew and trusted Acacius. He showed up when he said he would and he did what he said he would do, anyone's definition of a good builder.

Tetisheri stacked the paperwork dealing with the house construction in a tidy pile and set it to one side. "The new freighters?"

Neb beamed. "The first is due off the ways in two weeks."

"Our weeks or Caesar's weeks?"

Neb rolled his eyes. "Caesar's." His chest puffed out.

She chuckled. "You look like a proud father."

He grinned. "I feel like one, too. Do you want to see her?"

"Of course."

"Excellent. We'll go this afternoon."

"How is Demetrius' budget holding up?" Demetrius was the boatbuilder charged with expanding niche trader Nebenteru's Luxury Goods into a Middle Sea mercantile shipping power.

"Amazingly well." They conferred over the accounts for the freighters and even Tetisheri, who had a tendency to nitpick, admitted that they looked healthily on time and on budget.

Neb sat back with a sigh. "I'll be happy when we're out of the building business and back into the shipping business." He fingered the large, teardrop-shaped pearl woven into the tip of his pointed black beard. "Did you hear anything about a silphium shortage on your travels?"

Tetisheri raised an eyebrow. "No. Why?"

He tossed her a letter. "From Timur."

"Our factor in Cyrene?" She scanned the letter. Timur's written Greek was grammatically sloppy but perfectly understandable. "He can't find any silphium? In Cyrenaica?" She looked up. "The only place it grows?"

He nodded. "I know. Look at the date."

She looked. "August?"

"And I've heard nothing from him since."

Two months and more. She set the letter down. "That's not good. He's always been reliable."

"All our factors are reliable or they wouldn't be our factors." At her raised eyebrow, he deflated a little. "Apologies, Tetisheri. I know what you mean." He sighed. "It's just that Timur has been with us a long time. I'd hate to think—"

His voice died away but she understood what had been left unsaid. The good will of their business relied on the ability and probity of their closest associates. She picked up the letter again. "He says the farmers say silphium is getting harder to find." She frowned. "What does that mean, exactly? I'm no farmer, but I thought you sowed a plant, you watered and weeded it while it grew, and you harvested it in season and sent it off for sale."

He waved a hand. "So did I. All I know—all I need to know—is how much is delivered and how soon they can get it to me." He closed his eyes briefly and shook his head. "I can only imagine what Ephraim and Judoc will have to say to this."

Ephraim and Judoc being the two largest spice merchants in Alexandria and longtime customers. If they couldn't buy their silphium from Neb and Tetisheri, they would find another importer, and perhaps not only for silphium.

The mania for silphium among merchants and consumers both was founded in the herb's allegedly universal applications—culinary, cosmetic, and pharmacological. It was delicious eaten, stalk and root. Its sap was used as a seasoning. It was lauded as a cure-all for every ailment from lyssa to haimorrhoides. It was claimed to be an aphrodisiac, and if an unwanted pregnancy resulted from the first application, a second could be used as an abortifacient. A wonder drug indeed, Tetisheri thought. She retained a healthy skepticism in the matter of wonder drugs.

"Possibly..." Nebenteru hesitated.

"What?"

"Well." He picked up an ebony stylus and fiddled with it. "The new freighter will need a shakedown cruise. I thought the two of us might take her to Cyrene." He saw her expression. "Just a short voyage. There and back again. A few days. A week at most. Long enough to find Timur and determine what he's been up to."

"And perhaps some silphium?"

"Well. Yes. There is that."

She laughed. "I'll ask Herself if she can do without me for a bit."

His expression brightened. "Really?"

She looked at him affectionately. "Really, Uncle."

He fiddled with the stylus again and spoke in a kind of mumble. "I thought perhaps you might have had enough of travel for the moment."

"Not with you, Uncle. Never with you." She rose to her feet and looked down at him. He was a large man, in reputation, in financial success, and in physical form, resembling nothing so much as a bear one might see at the Hippodrome on a Saturday. With all that, he still managed to exude an aura of kindness and goodness and utter reliability.

It struck her that this last quality was something he shared with Apollodorus. She had to hide a smile at what the reaction would be if she said so out loud. To him or to Apollodorus. "In the meantime, let's take a stroll through the Emporeum on our way to see Demetrius. Chat up Ephraim and Judoc and the merchants. See if this shortage is general."

He raised an eyebrow. "If we can't get it, no one can?"

She spread her hands. "Worth finding out one way or another. I don't much like the thought of having to make excuses to some of our oldest customers."

"Nor do I," he said with feeling. "In my experience it's the best way to lose them."

Tetisheri broke her fast in the new-made kitchen, freshly plastered and painted and sparkling clean. Phoebe boiled her an egg, served with dried apricots and a round of bread fresh from her brand new brick oven, exhibiting a pride that extended far beyond the simple meal. "You like your new kitchen then," Tetisheri said, cracking and peeling her egg, warm to the touch, white firm and the yolk sludgy, just the way she liked it. She sprinkled on a bit of salt and took a bite. "Yum."

Nebet poured her a cup of pomegranate juice, fresh squeezed, and the two of them regaled Tetisheri with all the hardships they had endured over the past weeks and the cold meals they had contrived to fend off starvation. There were some tart observations about Acacius as well but Tetisheri wasn't fooled. They liked him or they wouldn't be trying to feed him up. Him and that fool Darib and the rest of his crew.

"Any news yet of Herminia?"

It was impossible to keep a secret in this household, as Tetisheri knew well, and there would be hurt feelings and extended sulks if no answer at all was forthcoming. She temporized. "She is presently out of the city, visiting relatives. I expect we'll see her again soon enough."

"No way to keep Herminia off the stage," Nebet said in a flat tone that brooked no contradiction. Phoebe nodded vigorously in assent.

Tetisheri thought of the circumstances in which Herminia, the most celebrated actor of her age, had been found two months before, and repressed a shudder. She couldn't imagine any incentive strong enough to deliberately put herself back in the public eye after something like that. But then she wasn't an actor. Actors only came truly alive in front of an audience.

The conversation turned, or was determinedly turned by both Phoebe and Nebet, to Tetisheri's changed circumstances. "So." Phoebe looked at her across the counter, dark eyes bright with interest. Next to her stood Nebet with a similar expression. Both women were in their fifties but their age had not diminished their interest in the details of Tetisheri's private life, especially now that there was a man in it. "Any word from Apollodorus?"

The Order of the Owls chose this moment to irrupt into the kitchen and Tetisheri was never more grateful to them. The Owls were five orphans between the ages of eight and ten, by way of war and family tragedy forced onto the streets of the city and working as messengers for hire. One fine day in September they had rescued Tetisheri from being kidnapped. She had rescued them right back and now they were pages ostensibly employed in her household, but in reality undercover agents for the Eye of Isis.

"How have you been keeping while I was away?" she said, and was pleased when she was overwhelmed by a clamorous recounting of their many tasks on behalf of Neb, Keren, Nike, Phoebe, and Nebet, not to mention Acacius' crew, who had found the availability of reliable messengers paid by someone else irresistible. The crew at the boatyard, too, had made use of them. Construction, whether land-based or maritime, was evidently productive of work enough to keep everyone busy.

"Excellent," she said. "I'm glad to hear you haven't been getting lazy." And then laughed at the avalanche of protests. She was especially pleased when Agape joined in, as trust came hard to the girl and she had been the last to believe in Tetisheri's offer of full employment, regular meals, and a home off the streets. Today, successfully fighting off Narses' attempt to snatch the last piece of bread, Agape looked her age for the first time since Tetisheri had met her.

She finished her tea and nodded at Babak, who followed her into the hall. "A message for the palace."

Babak brightened. He was still young enough to be bedazzled by close association with royalty. She had been younger than he was now when she had first met Cleopatra at school, which might account for the fact that she always saw the woman first, not the queen, no matter how laden with regalia or absolute in authority. "Yes, lady?"

"Go to the side entrance, you know the one. Ask for Charmion. Say that I request a private audience with the queen this afternoon."

"Beg a word with Charmion," he said, nodding. "Humbly ask for a private audience with Cleopatra, Seventh of her Name, the Lady of the Two Lands, Queen of Alexandria and Egypt."

She thought about chastising him for the descriptors, and let it go. "You will attend me. I'll meet you at the door, an hour from now."

He gave her a shallow bow and dashed off, not to the front door, but to the Mews, as the Order of the Owls' quarters had been dubbed by Uncle Neb. There probably to change into clothes befitting the occasion, of which each Owl now had a set.

She returned to Uncle Neb's office, smiling. Bast looked up from washing a paw and gave an interrogative "Mrow?"

"Yes, it goes well." She thought again of Apollodorus and sighed. "Mostly."

Bast waited for her to sit down and leapt lightly into her lap. She curled into a black circle and began to purr, kneading Tetisheri's tunic. One of the claws pierced the fabric and Tetisheri jumped. "Ouch! Careful!"

Bast opened one blue eye to give her a considering look, and closed it again. The kneading stopped but the purr continued, steady, rumbling, and infinitely comforting.

The walk through the Emporeum was less satisfactory.

Their route took them past the slave market, a location Tetisheri shunned as much as she was able to while still getting business done. It occupied a small open square on the edge of the Canopic Way, just enough beneath the roof of the Emporeum to be protected from sun and rain but near enough to the street for the sales to be enjoyed by gossiping passersby, students from the Mouseion, scholars from the Library, merchants, housewives and slaves already sold and meant to be about their master's business.

This afternoon the selection was small and the auctioneer sweating in an effort to move stock. Tetisheri watched as he put an older Greek woman on display who had lost most of her teeth to successive beatings if her misshapen features were any guide. She was thin to the point of emaciation, probably because she had nothing left to chew with. "Not much to look at, admittedly," the auctioneer cried, "but, my good sirs and ladies, a cook of surpassing talent! Gifted with spices from garum to silphium, and a hand with sauces to rival Archestratus himself!"

"Why is she for sale, then?"

"Why, her master died, good sir, and his children have their own cooks. Come, what am I bid for this asset to any kitchen? Would you start at a denarius?"

If she wasn't sold here she would be sent to a mine or a farm or a tomb raising, worked until she dropped in her tracks, and buried in a common grave with those of her equally unlucky fellows. Nebenteru took a firm grip on Tetisheri's arm and steered her down the sidewalk until they were out of earshot. "We can't afford to buy every slave you feel sorry for, Sheri."

"I know, Uncle." And she did know, but it never stopped her wanting to. She took a deep breath and banished the scene from her mind. Or tried to. It helped that Agape had taken it upon herself to accompany them and strutted at Tetisheri's side wearing the Owl brooch on her shoulder with manifest pride. While Tetisheri was pleased that the girl was proud enough to boast of her employer, she worried that it would attract unwanted attention. The symbol of the Eye of Isis was instantly recognizable to every Greek, Egyptian, Jew, and foreigner in Alexandria and Egypt. The identity of the current holder of the Eye, while not strictly a state secret, was not publicized by the palace or indeed by Tetisheri herself. Her medallion of office she wore inside her tunic, ready to pull out at need, but a certain amount of anonymity was useful as inquiries went forth. She feared that as the Owls became known as an adjunct of the Eye, as they inevitably would, the brooch could make the wearer a target.

And then she gave herself a mental shake. The Owls had survived a harsh, hungry, homeless existence for years before she had found them—or they found her—and while they all shared a tendency to distrust and a propensity for nightmares it hadn't harmed either their intelligence or their self-reliance. They'd lost their parents long ago and such relatives as remained to them had long since cast them off. Babak had built them up one street urchin at a time into the fiercely loyal and independent group they were today. What they most wanted was her respect. Well, Bast knew they had that.

She found Agape staring up at her with what she could only describe as disapproval. "What?" she said.

"Where is Apollodorus, lady?"

"I beg your pardon?"

"You spend weeks away in his company and when you both return to Alexandria he is gone practically the next day."

Tetisheri raised an eyebrow. "Are you demanding to know Apollodorus' intentions, Agape?"

On her other side Uncle Neb turned a laugh into a cough and hastened forward. "Judoc!"

"Nebenteru, well met!" The tall, thin man with the elaborately curled earlocks and voluminous and stiffly starched black robe strode out to grasp both of Neb's hands in his own. The two men exchanged hearty backslaps, and Judoc looked over Neb's shoulder to incline his head at Tetisheri. She bowed as slightly back. She was unclear as to which particular sect Judoc belonged but had learned through long acquaintance that its beliefs precluded anything approaching familiarity with women outside it.

He acknowledged her existence but only just, and only out of his friendship with Neb.

He was a faithful customer, though. And Alexandria and her queen never turned anyone away who was good at creating income and willing—mostly—to pay taxes on it.

Judoc's shop was one of the Emporeum's permanent establishments, a small freestanding building with solid doors and a secure lock made of heavy bronze. Spices were expensive and small in size and a month's net income could disappear in a moment behind one carelessly turned back, or a shoddy lock.

The doors stood open now, looking out on the Canopic Way, revealing tables laden with large flat vessels supporting colorful, conical piles of spices ground and whole and herbs dried and fresh. In the back stood large crocks of garum and oils and vinegars. When the wind was in the right quarter the combined strength of those scents could bring an involuntary tear to the eye. What little free space there was was crammed with slaves and servants and housewives and cooks raising pinches of cumin and turmeric to their noses to check for freshness and bargaining for the best price with Judoc's bevy of clerks.

Judoc sent for refreshments. The clerk winked at Tetisheri as he passed her on his way out but then he was Greek and they were a naturally flirtatious race. With their gods as examples, it was no wonder.

Judoc offered Neb a stool inside a small room at the back, where the noise and smells of the Emporeum were at least somewhat subdued, and Tetisheri took a seat on the floor behind Uncle Neb, near enough to hear but not near enough to offend Judoc's delicate sensibilities. Agape settled in behind, Babak next to her. There followed a discussion on the state of Middle Sea trade, a comprehensive merchant's-eye view of the recent Alexandrian War and its deleterious effects on business, a compliment to Cleopatra the Builder's efforts to repair the city and bring it back into its own again following said war, Neb's home remodel—Neb promised an open house when construction was complete, but then throwing parties for his clients and customers was meat and drink for her uncle and Judoc would have expected no less—and the progress of the construction of the new cargo ships. Neb should know, said Judoc, that there was great interest among the merchants of the Emporeum in Neb's new venture and that he hoped Neb would keep his oldest clients in mind when Sea to Sea Imports—a fine, proud name that indicated the ambitions of its owners and, dare he mention, potential investors—he actually nodded a second time at Tetisheri, two acknowledgements of her existence in one audience, she hoped her heart could take it—when Sea to Sea Imports began to book new sailings and new cargoes. At this point the Greek, Myron by name, returned with a tray and Judoc poured tea, three cups, although Neb had to hand the third cup to Tetisheri so that Judoc's hand was not sullied by the touch of a female.

The tea was hot and strong and the savory rolls flavored with some of Judoc's own spices. Judoc accepted Neb's compliments graciously.

"And how goes the spice trade?" Nebenteru said, dusting crumbs from the front of his tunic.

Judoc's brow clouded. "Not as well as one could hope."

Neb was all concern. "Only tell me of your difficulties, my dear Judoc, and I will do my best to erase them from existence."

Judoc cocked an eyebrow at Neb. "At a profit, no doubt."

Neb grinned widely. "At a profit for both of us, I would hope."

Judoc laughed and raised his hand, acknowledging Neb's point. He sobered then, to speak with grave emphasis. "Supplies from the east have been limited since the war, and far too dear when they arrive here in Alexandria."

"I will send messages at once to my factor in Berenike," Uncle Neb said, with equal gravity. "I will have news within the month and, I hope, spices for you as well. Have your clerk draw up a list of those most wanted."

Judoc inclined his head. "Thank you, Nebenteru. Your service is much appreciated."

Uncle dismissed this compliment with a large-minded hand. "I suppose I have no need to ask after your supplies of the more common spices to be found closer to home." He tapped his nose. "I see Romans everywhere in the streets now that the Lady of the Two Lands has brokered at least a semblance of peace."

"There will be no peace until she puts Philo out of all our misery."

Judoc's voice had risen on this bitter comment, and Neb patted the air. "Softly, Judoc, softly. One never knows who is listening in Alexandria."

Judoc looked a little conscious and glanced around the small room, cramped with a desk piled high with paperwork and stools and themselves. "My apologies, my dear fellow. But he sends his people into the Emporeum and they seem to think they can take any amount of what they like and drop not a single drachma in exchange. The Lady's servants pay up on the spot and in full."

Philo being Ptolemy XIV, Cleopatra's brother, husband, and co-regnant in name and only according to the dictates of the Colossus of Rome, Julius Caesar himself. In truth, Cleopatra reigned alone and had borne Caesar a child that very year to cement their bargain.

Neb was all sympathy. "Appalling, Judoc, and nothing more than I would have expected, given his lack of character."

"He displays all the vices of that family and none of the virtues. He has no thought for his subjects, only for himself and his own power."

"Or lack of it, eh?"

Judoc laughed and the storm passed. "As you say, Nebenteru." He filled his cup and raised it. "To the health and long life of the Lady of the Two Lands."

Neb matched him. "Hear, hear." They drank and surreptitiously Tetisheri drank with them. Health and long life indeed.

Neb snapped his fingers. "I almost forgot. Judoc, have you any ferula? My cook wanted me to ask."

"Of course, of course, anything for Phoebe." Judoc nodded at the Greek clerk who disappeared into the shop. "Lucky she didn't ask for silphium. There is none to be had, not for love nor money."

"Since I'd have to exchange one of my new ships for a single stalk, I'll pass," Uncle Neb said very dryly.

Judoc's brow creased. "It's odd, that, Neb. When I was a boy silphium was easily found in every marketplace. Oh yes, it is the dearest of all herbs, no question, and with a range of uses, the least of which is as a seasoning for food. But then it was always easily available. Now it is almost impossible to find."

"Over-harvesting, perhaps? A victim of its own popularity?"

"Possibly. It grows only Cyrenaica, I'm told, and the Romans have had that province firmly tied to their tails for fifty years. I imagine if there is any to be had it will go straight to Rome. In fact I remember hearing Caesar keeps a store under lock and key in the treasury there. Ah, well." Judoc shrugged. "We shall have to make do with ferula."

"Phoebe will, at any rate." Neb got to his feet and gave Tetisheri a hand up. "Thank you for your hospitality, Judoc. I'm taking the first new ship for a trial run next month. I'll keep my eye out for anything hard to find in the way of spices and herbs."

Judoc barely nodded at Tetisheri. Tetisheri barely nodded back. Neb saluted him and they left.

Neb and Tetisheri strolled through the Emporeum, responding to greetings and stopping briefly to admire the new line of leather purses Chi had on display. Demetrius' shipyard was on the other side of Kibotos near to the Gate of the Moon, and the *Hapi II* stood high and proud on the ways and was duly admired in terms that made its builder beam with pride.

Neb and Tetisheri took their leave with expressions of mutual esteem. When they came to Hermes Street Neb paused. He was frowning. "What is it, Uncle?"

"You'll tell her what Judoc said about Philo?"

"Certainly. Although she'll know it already. I swear there is nothing of interest she doesn't know well before it comes to the attention of any other citizen of the city."

Neb still looked unhappy.

"Uncle. What troubles you?"

He stepped closer and spoke in a voice meant only for her ears. "The gods know I have no love for the kinglet."

Tetisheri had to repress a smile. The epithet had sprung from Apollodorus and had since become family shorthand.

"But the Ptolemies have spent three centuries slaughtering one another, and every assassination always leads to another war. We just came out of one such. I'd hate—"

Tetisheri held up a hand and he stopped. Speaking in a tone to match his own, she said, "If Caesar died today Philo would be dead tomorrow, no question. But Caesar lives, Uncle, and his is the hand holding the tiller that steers us all now."

He looked doubtful. "Even her?"

"Even her." Tetisheri grimaced. "I'm not saying she likes it. But she knows how to be patient." A smile quirked at the corners of her mouth. "And she did inveigle Philo out of the city and onto Antirrhodos. He is now, literally, constantly under her eye."

An answering smile spread across his face. "It was well and craftily done, I admit." He sighed. "Very well, Sheri." He kissed her cheek. "You'll be home for dinner?"

"If I don't want Phoebe to poison my food in future, yes."

He laughed and set off toward home. She, Agape, and Babak walked up to the Canopic Way, where Babak waved down a cabrio. A young woman behind a dappled gray with a neatly brushed mane and tail and shined hooves swerved out of the stream of traffic, dodging a donkey-drawn cart with a load of broken stone and nearly clipping a coach overloaded with scholars preoccupied by a debate so hot they didn't even notice how close to death they had come. She nipped in a handspan in front of a rival cabrio, who had plenty to say about that, and drew up smartly in front of them. "Where to, lady?"

They scrambled in and sat down. "The palace, if you please."

The cabria looked as if all her dreams had come true, the palace being halfway across the city and then some, thus guaranteeing a fat fare. The three of them were rocked back in the seat as she snapped the reins and the gray broke into a trot, barely missing a gilded chariot bearing a fat merchant and his ink-stained scribe, to take their place in the stream of carts, cabrios, wagons, chariots, and coaches crowding the east-bound lane of the Way.

2

The Royal Palace was no one building, being instead an oddly graceful jumble of many such, aggregated around the Royal Harbor all the way out to the end of Lochias and continuing on to the islands clustering near the end of that peninsula. The oldest building dated back to Ptolemy I and every Ptolemy since had added to the pile. The one thing the Ptolemies did well, other than familicide, was build civic structures to their own greater glory.

Well. And acquire them. Tetisheri remembered only too well how Otho's new mansion had been incorporated into the royal estate. She was certain everyone else who had been there that day remembered it too, especially Otho.

The palace glittered blindingly against the deep blue of the Middle Sea and as one approached, the colors of the exterior embellishments coalesced out of the background. They formed the shapes of all the Egyptian gods revered by the ruling family over the past three centuries. The more popular (or royalty approved, which amounted to the same thing) gods of their times were commemorated on the friezes and porticos and columns of each reign. The paintings and carvings were maintained by an army of artisans who had no other job than to create in the beholder an impulse to abase themselves immediately before the accumulated aura of three centuries' worth of Ptolemies and four millennia of Pharaohs.

As one would expect, the newest buildings featured Isis and Horus almost exclusively, as did the latest issue of coinage jingling in fortunate pockets, the banners snapping in the breeze from the corner of every roof, and the items displayed on every souvenir cart parked at every corner of the Canopic Way. Cleopatra, Seventh of Her Name, knew how to imprint a brand. Moreover, she reasoned, rightly in Tetisheri's opinion, that the more ways to earn money she could make available to the citizens of Alexandria and Egypt, the less likely they were to rebel against her rule. They hadn't, yet, which made her unique among Ptolemies. It was an achievement Cleopatra was determined to maintain.

That determination had everything to do with the Royal Guard's encampment that sat solidly between Lochias and the Royal Harbor and the rest of the city, filled with recruits from Pelusium to Syene, organized into an auxiliary legion and training under the aegis of the Roman army, which by any other name would read Julius Caesar. As they passed the training ground Tetisheri saw one brand new cohort in full armor in close order drill, all of whom looked sweaty and exhausted and three of whom fell on their faces at the command to halt. Someone had misbehaved, and the grizzled Roman in command, one of many Cleopatra had co-opted from the ranks of retired Roman legionnaires, looked disinclined to show mercy. At any rate, at his order the rest of the cohort marched right over the fallen and kept going.

The anonymous side door opened immediately to her knock and they were ushered inside by a member of Cleopatra's personal guard. Unlike the raw recruits they had just seen being hammered into shape, this man was older and supremely self-assured. "Hesperos. Well met this day."

His gaze stripped them of their clothes, found no weapons in so doing, and gave a slight bow. "Well met, lady. This way, if you please."

She started to follow him and felt a hand tug at her tunic. She turned. "Us, too?" Babak said in a stage whisper.

"You, too." She was hoping that more interaction with the queen would dull the edges of their propensity for idolatry. Cleopatra might deliberately embody herself as the avatar of Isis on earth for the masses but the Owls worked for the Eye of Isis, and the current Eye had no time to waste on bootlicking. The more exposure they had to Cleopatra the woman, the less inclined they would be to fall dumbstruck in her presence. She hoped.

She turned and followed Hesperos without looking back. After a moment she heard the sound of footsteps, although the Owls were too intimidated even to whisper. That or they were memorizing the route, which took some doing. The strenuous remodeling to make the three buildings down on Hermes Street into one had nothing on the rabbit warren that resulted when each of fifteen Ptolemies insisted on building something bigger and better than the one who came before them. And, naturally, all of these buildings had to be connected, as their delicate royal selves could not be asked to suffer the harsh elements of the outside world. Translated into *lingua conventus*, this meant that the less they exposed themselves to the murderous mobs that had knocked at all their doors save one, the better pleased and, more importantly, the longer lived they'd be.

Deep inside the bowels of the royal beast, Hesperos stopped beside a double door and motioned them inside.

The doors opened into a large room used by the head of state to conduct public business out of the public eye. It was square in shape with a high ceiling and only a Greek key frieze running around the walls just beneath the ceiling for adornment. It was a frieze merely painted on, not sculpted from stone or marble. It was as plain as Alexandrian architecture got and its very anonymity made a statement to all in attendance: state your business, stick to the point, no whining at the judgement, and get out.

Outside of Cleopatra's private quarters, it was Tetisheri's favorite room in the palace. This was the room where everything of importance happened, distinguished from any one of the several elaborately furnished, blindingly over-gilded throne rooms where the queen received ambassadors, generals, her nobles, and the nobility of lands that did not lie beneath the authority of the crook and flail. Of necessity they must be humbled by the outward appearance of as many of the treasures of Alexandria and Egypt as a Ptolemy could assemble in one place. Which was quite a lot, none of which was comfortable to sit on.

In this room, Cleopatra wore no royal regalia, only a

simple linen sheath and plain leather sandals, no jewelry, no wig. Her hair looked ruffled, as if she'd been running her hands through it, and her skin was free of cosmetics. Her table was, admittedly, made of ebony, with the legs carved in the shapes of elephants sitting up, trunks raised to bear the weight of the top, but otherwise you'd never have known she wasn't just another one of the clerks.

That is, if you didn't take into account the abject deference shown her by everyone else in the room. Her table sat at the center of other, more utilitarian tables, made of unvarnished acacia, each of them manned by two or more clerks. Every table was piled high with papyri and everyone's work was continually interrupted by a stream of more clerks coming and going, bearing arms full of more documents and carrying others away. Messengers dashed in and out bearing letters and reports and petitions. Some stayed for a reply; most departed instantly with an air of relief. Propinquity with Ptolemies was not conducive to a long life, and while Cleopatra had proved herself less bloody-minded than her royal ancestors, she still had a lot to prove to a population who remembered very clearly the battles of the recent war being fought outside their front doors.

Cleopatra's table was bare by comparison to those of her many clerks, as the reports and petitions that reached her had been vetted first by the secretaries of the various nomes, approved by the nomarch, and scrutinized by Horemheb, her secretary for internal affairs. He occupied no table, but moved from one to another, scrutinizing the work of the clerks over their shoulders. They were so used to his frowning presence they didn't even cower. Occasionally he pointed at some phrase or signature, asked a question, and listened to the answer. Rarely he bore the document in question to the queen for her personal attention.

Charmion stood at Cleopatra's shoulder. She seldom spoke. When she did she was always attended to by both queen and secretary.

As if Charmion could feel Tetisheri's gaze she looked up. Tetisheri raised an eyebrow and Charmion looked back at the document Horemheb had only just set before the queen. Tetisheri had excellent hearing and she didn't bother pretending not to listen to their low-voiced conversation.

Cleopatra spoke in an entirely neutral tone, no hint of what she was feeling one way or another. "I believe this is now the second year in a row Ennius has claimed reimbursement for construction of the aqueduct in Tebtynis."

"Yes, Majesty."

"Tebtynis, where he lives."

"Well." Horemheb contemplated his feet. "Say rather, Majesty, that is where his property resides. I believe he spends most of his time here in the city."

"He has a tenant farmer in Tebtynis?"

"He does." Horemheb consulted his notes. "One Hori."

Cleopatra sat back and tapped her chin with an ink-stained finger. "Ennius would be a retired legionnaire?"

"A centurion, Majesty. Of the Third Gallica."

The Third Gallica had been established by Caesar himself. Veterans of the Third were among Caesar's most well-rewarded beneficiaries, particularly of lands belonging to other, non-Roman people. "Who makes this request? Hori, or Ennius?"

"Ennius. Both times."

"Ah." Cleopatra sat forward again. "Write to Hori. Ask

him for the particulars of the matter. Specifics, Horemheb—who is the engineer, who is the architect, from where to where is the route. A cost list, enumerated. Copy Ennius, and tell him as soon as we are in possession of all the facts we will render our judgement in the matter. Horemheb?" This as the royal secretary began to turn. Cleopatra smiled. "Be sure to add my personal felicitations and best wishes for the continued good health of Ennius and all his family."

"Majesty." Wooden-faced, Horemheb effaced himself and returned the petition to the clerk whence Ennius' letter had come.

"Is that the last of it, Charmion?"

"For today, Majesty."

"Isis bless us all." She stood up and stretched. Styli and papyrus cascaded to the floor as every clerk leaped to his or her feet. "Sit down and back to work with you!" She pretended to notice Tetisheri for the first time. "My lady Tetisheri. Well met."

Tetisheri approached and bowed. "Majesty."

"Always a pleasure to see you again, lady." Cleopatra smiled at her and then at Babak, bowing next to her. "And this is—Babak? Have I got that right?"

Babak tried to look at her without straightening up, when it was perfectly obvious he wanted to fall flat in abject obeisance. His queen had actually remembered his name. "Majesty."

"And this is—" Cleopatra indicated Agape, next to Babak.

"Agape, Majesty," Agape said before Tetisheri could say anything. She touched her fingertips to heart, lips, and forehead in graceful salute while performing a practiced bow that would have shamed many a professional courtier. "Your most devoted servant."

Tetisheri and Cleopatra and Charmion all looked at Agape with varying degrees of surprise. Babak outright gaped at her. Evidently there was more to Agape's story than even he knew.

Cleopatra recovered first. "I see you are both wearing your badge of office. Owls, who hunt by night. Very appropriate. Nicely crafted, too." She looked at Tetisheri. "Matan?"

Tetisheri nodded. "It was a small thing, and not something he usually does, but he obliged me."

"Lucky you."

Tetisheri gave her a sharp look, but the queen did not meet her eyes, instead directing a warm smile at the two Owls. "I expect you're hungry. Charmion, take them to the kitchens to see what you can find, and then bring them to my sitting room."

"Majesty." Charmion and the Owls went in one direction and Tetisheri and Cleopatra in another. They said no more until they'd reached the queen's private quarters, where Cleopatra was met by Iras, who clucked with disapproval and whisked her most royal highness forthwith to the bath. There she was sluiced free of ink and clad in clean clothes and returned to her sitting room with a stern admonition.

"One hour before the reception, Majesty. I will return in half that to help you dress."

"I hear and obey," Cleopatra said to her back as it disappeared behind the door, which closed firmly behind her.

Cleopatra nodded at the door that led onto the balcony

that overlooked the Royal Harbor. "I could use some fresh air. I'll pour us a drink."

A gentle breeze moved the translucent gauze curtains to one side as Tetisheri stepped through. The sun glittered on the waves and threw light shadows against the walls of the Royal Palace and against the massive tower of the Pharos opposite it. All evidence of construction had been tidied away and it looked as impervious to wind and weather and man as it had before the depredations of the Alexandrian War. To the left and a little behind the Heptastadion crossed the water between the Isle of Pharos and the city, separating the Port of Eunostos from the Great Harbor. It hosted the usual crowd of slaves and citizens hurrying to and fro. They were outnumbered two to one by tourists, mostly from Athens and Rome but representing people of every color, age, gender, shape, size, and race in the known world. Everyone came to Alexandria.

And many of them wanted to buy spices in the Grand Emporeum, Tetisheri thought. Including silphium.

The curtains rustled and Cleopatra joined her on the balcony, bearing a tray and two cups. "Sit, sit," the queen said, doing so herself. "What brings you under my eye today, Sheri?" She raised her cup in a toast, which Tetisheri matched. It was iced fruit juice, some kind of citrus unknown to her.

"Only the wish to bask in the radiance of your presence, O most high."

"Tchaa!"

Tetisheri chuckled. "Where's the baby?"

"Asleep, thank the gods. When, I ask myself, will he do something more than eat, sleep, and mess his clouts?"

Tetisheri raised an eyebrow. "It's not like you have to change them."

Cleopatra looked down her nose. "There are some royal prerogatives that make the crown less burdensome, it is true."

Tetisheri laughed and Cleopatra held out her hand to take Tetisheri's in a warm clasp. "How goes the remodel, Sheri?"

"Acacius tells us a few days more only, Pati, before we are rid of him."

"Builders." Cleopatra shook her head. In the ambitious, ongoing rebuild of Alexandria following the war, she knew more than her share and was only too familiar with their good attributes as well as their bad. "And Uncle Neb?"

"Flourishing."

"As always, but it is good to hear it said nonetheless." They paused when Iras brought a small plate of savory rolls still steaming from the oven. "And the new ships?"

"The first one comes off the ways in two weeks or so, Majesty." She waited until Iras had left them again. "It is why I came to see you, Pati. Neb wants to take her out for a shakedown cruise, and he wants me to come. I am to ask you if you can possibly do without my services for a short voyage."

"Where to?"

"Cyrene."

"Cyrene?"

Tetisheri nodded. "Silphium seems to be in short supply these days, and the spice merchants in the Emporeum are getting restless. Uncle Neb wrote to inquire of our factor in Cyrene some time ago and he hasn't heard back."

"And Neb is getting restless, too," Cleopatra said with a twinkle.

Tetisheri laughed. "You know him well."

Cleopatra folded her hands and rested her chin on them. "Cyrene, hmmm?"

"Yes. The coast of Cyrene is where silphium grows."

"Yes, I know. You should look up Theophrastus' writings on the subject. He visited Cyrene himself, and he wrote a great deal about silphium. It is a plant with odd habits."

Tetisheri looked up and spoke to the sky, or perhaps the gods eavesdropping beyond. "As long as I've known you, I should stop being surprised by the things you know. I will hie myself to the Library and speak fair of Sosigenes, that he might seek out this musty old tome for the wisdom it holds." She drained her cup and set it down. "Do I have your leave to lay down my badge of office for a few days? A week at most?"

"Umm. No. No, I'm afraid not."

Tetisheri narrowed her eyes and the queen laughed. "Don't look so suspicious, Sheri! No, it is that I find I have an errand for you, if you would be so kind." She smiled. "In Cyrene, as it happens."

Tetisheri sat back and contemplated her friend of many years and her employer of four months. "I know that look."

Cleopatra's eyes widened to their fullest extent. "What look?"

Tetisheri pointed her finger. "That one, that look right there. Are there any tombs cluttering up this errand? Any new construction? Any coinage in large amounts?"

Cleopatra held up her hands in mock horror. "A note to a

friend, Sheri, on my honor as Lady of the Two Lands!" She tsked. "You're so untrusting."

"Not untrusting. Just experienced."

The queen laughed again. "No, no, this time it is simply a letter to a friend."

"And this friend is—?"

Cleopatra smiled. "Cornelia Metella." She popped a roll into her mouth.

A brown slash against the sky made both women turn, and they watched a sparrow hawk streak down to catch an oblivious thrush in midair. There was a burst of feathers and a cry cut short as the sparrow hawk turned on the tip of one wing and began to beat its way back to its nest, which was probably on the Pharos. The raptors of Alexandria viewed the 350-foot high Pharos as prime real estate.

"Cornelia Metella," Tetisheri said, watching the small hawk clutching the smaller bird in its claws until it was out of sight. "Pompey's wife."

"Pompey's widow."

"She's in Cyrene?"

"Yes."

"But Caesar gave her Pompey's ashes and his ring and sent her home to Italy."

"Caesar sent Pompey's ring to Rome and had it put on display because none of those idiots would believe Pompey was dead." Cleopatra's voice was very dry. "And while Cornelia's husband is dead, her brother is still very much alive."

Tetisheri winced. "Metellus Scipio?"

"Indeed."

"And he's in Cyrene?"

"He is presently at Juba's court, bribing and bullying support."

"What happened to Varus?"

"At Cato's behest, as I understand it, Varus resigned his post to Scipio."

They were silent together for a moment, contemplating this latest calamity.

"Against Caesar. Metellus Scipio." And then just to underline her thought, she repeated the name. "Metellus Scipio." She was unable to moderate her disgust, but then she wasn't trying that hard.

"One of the most corrupt, debauched, amoral Romans living, and given the current crop, I agree, that's saying something." Cleopatra sounded almost amused but the look in her eye was anything but. "It's almost like the Pompeiians want to lose."

"And of course Juba would go to his grave opposing Caesar anyway. That whole beard-pulling thing." And Caesar, as was his invariable habit, had slept with Juba's wife. Probably best not to mention that in present company, although Cleopatra had never displayed any proprietary feelings toward the father of her child. Not openly, at any rate. "I don't recall Cornelia and Scipio ever being that close."

"They aren't. But her stepson, Sextus Pompey—"

"Oh Pati. No."

The queen gave a grim nod. "Sextus Pompey has joined Scipio in Cyrene. Cato, meantime, is on the Carthaginian peninsula with the garrison from Dyrrachium, in company with the other Pompeiians who refuse to accept that they're beat."

"Labienus?"

"And Afranius and Petreius. They've built up a considerable force."

"And Gnaeus?"

Gnaeus Pompey was Sextus Pompey's older brother. Cleopatra nodded. "Yes, he's there, too, although it's my understanding that Sextus is by far more valuable to the Pompeiians. Young as he is, he is reputed to be a capable naval commander." She gave a faint sigh. "I believe Cornelia followed them in hopes of convincing Sextus at least to make peace with Caesar."

Tetisheri raised an eyebrow. Julius Caesar only ever forgave once. Crossed a second time, he was implacable.

"Yes, I know. But he wept when they showed him Pompey's head. As for Cornelia, Pompey might have been the husband she actually cared for."

"He was thirty years older than she was."

"Nevertheless. Evidently at the very least she sees this as a duty she owes him."

"You'd think she'd be grateful to have survived her usefulness as a bargaining chip and just go home."

Cleopatra glanced at her, and Tetisheri tried to get her face and voice back under control. Even with Pati, there were wounds Tetisheri would not allow to be touched. "How many troops does Scipio have?"

"Between the remnants of Pompey's army and whatever conscripts Juba can throw together, if he so chooses? I don't know. I'd like to."

So would Caesar, Tetisheri thought, and wondered what, exactly, her true task was, and for whom. "You say you want me to carry a letter to Cornelia. It does just occur to me that your—relationship—with Julius Caesar might not give you the best entree into her good graces."

Cleopatra gave a faint smile. "My relationship with Cornelia predates my relationship with Caesar. I have nothing to fear there. Besides, Caesar didn't kill Pompey."

"No. Your brother did."

Cleopatra was imperturbable. "True, but irrelevant."

"If you say so."

Cleopatra patted Tetisheri's hand. "Don't worry, Sheri. She won't hand you your head when you walk through the door bearing my insignia."

"If you say so," Tetisheri said grimly, but was forced to smile when Cleopatra laughed.

She was not naive enough to imagine for one moment that carrying a message to Cornelia would be the end of it. Cleopatra would want a full briefing on the state of Juba's intentions toward Scipio and in particular the size of the forces he was willing to commit to Scipio's support against Julius Caesar. Juba was a notorious cloak-switcher and if Caesar could buy him off it could write a line once and for all beneath the Pompeiians' ambitions. So far they had proved themselves as easy to catch as the greased pig at the fair. And Caesar, let's not forget, had triumphs in Rome to plan in which he would demonstrate the greater glory of the power of Rome and, not coincidentally, his own.

If Juba could bought off, Tetisheri knew who would be footing that bill.

"Take the kids," Cleopatra said.

Tetisheri dragged her attention five hundred leagues back east. "What kids?"

The queen motioned toward the door. "Those two Owls."

43

"What?" Tetisheri stared. "Why?"

"They impressed me, and reliable messengers are always useful. Oh, and take two of the Soldiers with you."

"Soldiers" in this context could only mean two of the Five Soldiers, the co-owners and operators of the Five Soldiers Gymnasium. With awful sarcasm Tetisheri said, "I thought you said I'd be in no danger."

There was a stirring outside the door and Cleopatra rose to her feet. "With two of the Soldiers with you, you won't be. I suggest Isidorus. He's always good in a rough-and-tumble. And Dubnorix, who can hold his own among the patricians. Crixus and Castus are well able to manage the business while they're gone."

"Pati." Tetisheri hesitated. This came perilously close to trading on their friendship, but she wanted so badly to know. "Where is Apollodorus?"

Tetisheri could not read Cleopatra's expression. "He is about the queen's business," was all the Lady of the Two Lands would say.

The door opened on Iras, wearing a stern expression. "Majesty, it is time."

"Yes, yes, I come." To Tetisheri she said, "Iras is like the man with the flag at the Hippodrome, the one who starts all the races."

"And lucky for you I am, Majesty."

Over Iras' shoulder, Cleopatra winked at Tetisheri.

Tetisheri turned to leave, only to hear the queen call her name. "I've just had a thought."

"Yes, Majesty?"

"You might like to visit Calliope."

Tetisheri stared. "Calliope? The hetaira?"

"Yes. I hear she has a new patron."

"And?"

"One new come from Cyrenaica."

Iras began to close the door and through its rapidly disappearing opening she heard Cleopatra say, "It wouldn't hurt to pick up some of the latest gossip before you go. Iras, give over, I come, I come!"

3

He heard the rhythm of their marching feet when they turned onto his street, but that was only because he'd been listening for it for so long. In spite of having known it was coming for weeks and even months now, in spite of moving his wives and children to safety along with all their more valuable possessions, in spite of having made this decision long since and soberly and realistically counting its inevitable cost, he could not stop the tremble that began deep in his gut and spread throughout his body.

He steadied himself against his desk for a moment, and then went with a firm tread out through the atrium to unbar the door. He knew they would be angry and get only angrier, and he wanted to avoid as much destruction to his home as possible. His wives might be able to sell it one day.

It was a vain hope. They entered quietly enough from the outside gloom of a late summer's night, slammed him onto the bench next to the fountain, and then went through every room in the villa with the brutal efficiency of experienced plunderers. Every cushion and mattress was ripped open, what containers remained in every cupboard emptied onto the floor, murals were defaced. He found a moment to grieve over the one showing Cleopatra with Caesarion, beautiful, smiling mother and laughing, rosy-cheeked babe in arms, their eyes now gouged out at sword's point. Holes were kicked in the walls where hiding places were suspected. Outside he heard them in the back garden, the sound of blades being thrust into the ground, searching for anything that might be buried there.

It wasn't long before they were done. Their leader, a man he had drunk with, a man he had invited into his home, a man who had brought rare delicacies to his wives and toys to his children, this man now knelt before him on one knee. "Well, now, friend."

In spite of himself he almost laughed. He had no friends here.

"I have only one question. Where is it?"

His voice was shaky and he made no attempt to strengthen it. "Where is what? I don't know why you're here or what you're talking about."

"Which would be why the house is stripped and your family gone."

"They're in the country visiting my first wife's mother."

"And you didn't go with them?"

He didn't have to pretend to shudder. "She's a harridan. My mother-in-law. I pled work to excuse my absence.

Believe me, she'll be as happy I wasn't there as I was not to go."

A deep chuckle. "Don't I know the type." He looked up and around. "Don't we all."

His companions' silence was oddly terrifying, as if to signal their indifference to anything he might say.

"Where in the country?"

He answered readily, having practiced the story in anticipation of this day. "Arsinoë. She's a widow. No surprise. Her husband left his farm there to her."

"Arsinoë. Arsinoë. Hmm."

There was a brief silence. For one fleeting moment he thought he might live to see the sun rise again.

But then the man rose to his feet. "Plausible, I grant you. But I find myself unconvinced. And there is the matter of what is missing here, of which, strangely, you make no mention. No." He said it firmly, if regretfully, and turned his head to the figure nearest him in the gloom.

"Gag him first. We don't want to wake up the neighbors."

4

Many things to do and a mere fourteen days to get them done. That night House Nebenteru rang with Uncle's joy that the two of them would together embark on a voyage for the first time since the war. Off they would go, he said, with expansive gestures, far away from the intrigues of Alexandria's divided courts and the restlessness of Alexandria's citizens, whose propensity for protest over the least little thing could never be underestimated.

As in truth Cleopatra never did, but no one could help but notice (especially Alexandrians, and even more specifically the Alexandrian Greeks) that she spent an equal amount of time with her citizens of Egypt. They had been welcomed into the city with arms opened more widely than any Ptolemy had ever done. It was certainly remarkable how many of the river folk had flocked to the banner of the

Royal Guard, and it was in fact remarked on in every house and marketplace. The fact that immigration into the city had been made lawful by their queen and goddess didn't stop the Alexandrian Greeks from grumbling about it.

Alexandria was the largest, the most beautiful, and the most modern city on the Middle Sea. But it was not a peaceful one.

Tetisheri was careful not to tell Neb of the queen's tasking her with carrying a message to Cornelia. It would have destroyed much of his pleasure in their escape, however temporary.

The next morning Tetisheri hied herself off to the Great Library, where a grumbling Sosigenes rooted out a copy of Theophrastus translated into contemporary Greek. She took herself and the scroll to a carrel and with pen and papyrus noted down what that learned man had had to say about silphium nearly three hundred years before.

It turned out in at least this agricultural instance, cultivation was not after all a matter of planting a seed and standing back out of its way. Silphium grew wild or it didn't grow at all. Interesting. It was also fussy about when it was harvested and for which part, as root, stem, leaf, seed, sap, and flower all appeared to be useful for something, from medicine to cosmetics to the culinary arts.

> The Libyans know the season for cutting, for it is they that gather the silphium. So also do the rootdiggers and those that collect medicinal juices, for these too tap the stems earlier. And in general all those who collect whether roots or juices observe the season which is appropriate in each case.

Tetisheri wondered which part of the plant was purposed for its aphrodisiacal properties. She wondered, too, if it was true that Caesar kept his supply locked away in Rome's treasury. Given the lecherous swath he cut through Europe and all around the Middle Sea, if it truly did increase desire the wonder was he saw no need to bring it with him.

Although Caesar's reputation for satyriasis was such that she had to admit it didn't sound as if he needed any assistance.

Theophrastus said further that livestock, too, enjoyed the taste of silphium, and that it made their milk more sweet and their meat more tender. She wondered what effect it had on their mating habits.

She resolutely avoided being sidetracked into the natural philosopher's digressions into capers, almonds, and cumin, although she might have made a mental note of where to find those passages at some later date.

She went to the room where the Library's thousands of drawings were kept filed and indexed, where she was delighted to find many of silphium by various and sundry philosophers, including Theophrastus. Silphium held a fascination for many, it seemed. She had a clerk make tracings of the three of the best—it was certainly an unlovely plant, resembling nothing so much as the forced mating of Osirus and Sobek's crowns circa the Tenth Dynasty— returned the drawings to the room's custodian and brought her notes and tracings home. Acacius et al were still on the roof, and later the crew stood in line for Phoebe and Nebet to fill their bowls.

"Maybe we should start charging them for their meals," Keren said over spicy lamb and bean stew that evening.

Nike, House Nebenteru's self-appointed steward, snorted her agreement. "They'll never finish the roof so long as we keep feeding them."

Neb looked guilty.

The next day Tetisheri went to the Five Soldiers, east of Lochias off the Canopic Way. Rhode drove her, and she did not go empty-handed, as Phoebe and Nebet had been busy in the kitchen the entire previous afternoon. There were dolmas, of course, and succulent meat pies, and tangy fruit tarts, and an amphora of a very nice Greek wine of a size to tickle everyone's palate but not enough to get anyone drunk. Tetisheri was not giving Is and Dub any excuse to say she had taken advantage of them while they were incapacitated. When they heard they had been chosen by the queen herself to accompany Tetisheri on her mission they bowed to the inevitable, although Crix and Cas did sulk a bit at being left behind.

Much time was spent over the following days canvassing the merchants in the Emporeum for anything they might like Neb's new ship to bring them from ports west. Demetrius the Shipwright put in an order for all the oak they could find, as Sea to Sea Imports was stretching his stores pretty thin. Or, as he put it, "Your uncle has skinned out my warehouse like a gazelle under the butcher's knife. If he wants the *Hapi III* to come off the ways on schedule he'd better start filling it back up again."

The day before the blocks were scheduled to be knocked out from beneath the hull of the *Hapi II*, Tetisheri remembered what Cleopatra had said about Calliope's new patron and paid a courtesy call on the most famous and successful hetaira in Alexandria. She had been tried for impiety before the Senate of Rome and upon her decidedly debatable acquittal had wisely abandoned the north shore of the Middle Sea for the south. They had met in the course of the second investigation Tetisheri had undertaken as the Eye of Isis. Since then she had cultivated Calliope as a source of information, and possibly as a friend.

Although Tetisheri generally trusted her friends and she didn't trust Calliope as far as her own front door.

"My lady Tetisheri." Calliope, slender to the point of thinness, with a rope of hair almost as big around as her waist and large, thickly lashed eyes made for flirting, bowed slightly. "Well met on the day."

"Well met, lady. Thank you for being at home to me."

Calliope might have smiled. "One must always be at home to such a dear friend of our queen."

Tetisheri had a high respect for Calliope's intelligence—one must never forget that acquittal—and she was certain that Calliope knew Tetisheri was more than just Cleopatra's friend. When they had both sipped of the tea a maid brought on a tray, she said, "As it happens, tomorrow my uncle and I make the maiden voyage of his newest cargo ship."

Calliope nodded. "All in the city hears of the expansion of House Nebenteru's home and business ventures. It must be very exciting."

"As you say." Tetisheri smiled. "However, one does not wish to sail off into the unknown if one can help oneself."

"Indeed not. May one ask if the unknown has a name?"

Tetisheri saw the twinkle in the other woman's eye and laughed. "A brief voyage, only, a week or ten days' round trip if all goes well. To Cyrene. Which is why I am here."

Calliope seemed to stiffen ever so slightly, enough to

give Tetisheri pause. "Have I said something to upset you, lady?"

The hetaira smiled, an expression that looked forced to Tetisheri, who was now watching her very closely. "No indeed, lady. Cyrene. A lovely city. Nothing to compare with Alexandria, of course."

Tetisheri looked hard at her, but Calliope only raised one eyebrow in polite inquiry. Tetisheri, however, remained on the alert. "I have no very recent news of Cyrene." She sipped her tea again, allowing the words to drop delicately into the pool of expectant silence and ripple gently across to the woman in the chair across from her. "All of the city knows of the lady Calliope's vast treasury of friends." She cocked her head. "Not to mention her almost uncanny ability to hear all the news first, whether from home or abroad."

"Do they. How very flattering." The hetaira had recovered her composure. She folded her hands and tapped her thumbs together, as adept as Tetisheri at letting a silence be felt. "As it happens, not long ago I spoke to a dear friend only recently returned from Cyrene."

Tetisheri inclined her head. "How fortuitous. What had he to say?"

Calliope's eyes wandered around her sitting room, lingering for a moment on a small, exquisite statue of Aphrodite painted so beautifully in rich blues and greens that it seemed to glow with an inner light from where it stood on a highly polished ebony plinth. Both were new since Tetisheri's last visit, and she would have bet her half of Sea to Sea Imports that Calliope had paid the same price for them as she had for every other precious object in the room. A treasury of friends, indeed.

"What had my dear friend to say of Cyrene?" Calliope said at last, looking back at Tetisheri. "Much of interest."

When Calliope seemed disinclined to expand on that thought, Tetisheri possessed her soul in patience and prodded by hazarding a guess. "Does Cyrene entertain foreign visitors, perhaps?"

If she hadn't been watching the other woman so closely, she might have missed the slight, brief widening of the other woman's eyes.

"As it happens, you are correct. In bulk, according to my informant." Calliope raised her cup to her lips and pretended to sip. She set the cup down again, every movement as always a lesson in grace, and raised guileless eyes to Tetisheri's face. "One wonders at the queen's interest in a place so far away."

Tetisheri raised polite eyebrows in return, ignoring the many obvious responses to that comment, given that Cyrene was right next door to Egypt and already firmly locked into the Roman yoke Cleopatra was so determined to avoid. "The queen's interest? Say rather mine and my uncle's. As I said, we are taking our first new ship on its maiden voyage, and Cyrene is an easy sail."

Calliope raised her own eyebrows in polite disbelief and in spite of herself Tetisheri laughed out loud. "Very well. It is true, Uncle Neb and I never go anywhere for only one reason." She leaned forward and dropped her voice to a conspiratorial murmur, noting with some satisfaction that Calliope leaned forward to meet her halfway. "The spice merchants in the Emporeum complain of a shortage of silphium. Silphium comes from Cyrene, so we had thought to inquire once we were there."

"Ah." Calliope sat back and smoothed the fine linen of her tunic over her knees with an oddly focused determination. Not that any conversation with Calliope could be called straightforward, but this one had seemed ever so slightly off since Tetisheri first mentioned Cyrene.

"Silphium," Calliope said. "Yes, Phryne says our cook has complained of not being able to lay hands on any for any price."

Phryne being the single-headed Cerberus who was Calliope's steward.

"There are many Romans resident in Juba's court at present, according to my dear friend." She raised her eyes to meet Tetisheri's, and the expression in them could not have been more bland. "Including Metellus Scipio and his nephews, Gnaeus Pompey and Sextus Pompey. It seems they sought sanctuary at Juba's court following the unfortunate outcome of the battle of Pharsalus."

"Unfortunate for them."

"As you say. More tea?"

"Please."

"And you must try one of these savory biscuits. Your cook—Phoebe, isn't it?—would surely be intrigued."

The biscuit was satisfyingly crunchy and tangy with cheese and herbs. "Delicious. Phoebe will be delighted if your cook—Korinna, isn't it?—can be persuaded to share the recipe."

The corners of Calliope's lips deepened but only momentarily. "Perhaps they should meet."

"Perhaps." Tetisheri set her cup down with the respect due to a piece of pottery exemplifying the best of Corinthian art, and wondered which *amans diei* was responsible for its presence in this house.

She looked up to meet Calliope's carefully pleasant gaze. She could have blushed to have been caught with her thoughts so plain on her face. Instead, she grinned and shrugged. "One hears such tales. It is difficult not to be curious."

Infinitesimally Calliope seemed to relax a trifle more. "At least you're honest about it."

Tetisheri indicated the cup. "It's a lovely piece."

"Thank you." Calliope drained her cup and set it down in turn. "Scipio is jogging Juba's elbow. Juba is being his usual charming and duplicitous self." She hesitated. "My dear friend reports a rumor abroad in Cyrene." She looked up to meet Tetisheri's eyes. "That Caesar's agents are present there as well."

Tetisheri snorted. "Did they bring money?"

Calliope smiled. "He can barely pay his troops. But I'm sure he would have plenty on hand for Juba, if he thought Juba would accept it." Her smile faded. "There is another rumor as well, although my dear friend stressed that his informant in this matter was unreliable." She picked at an invisible piece of lint on her knee. "The rumor is that Bocchus has sent a representative to treat with Juba."

"Bocchus? Not Bogud?"

Calliope's voice was very dry. "The brothers have, as usual, been very careful to keep a foot in both camps."

"So they'll be on the winning side no matter what."

"Exactly." Calliope gave a faint sigh. "The drums of war begin to sound again. They are at present faint, but there is no mistaking that sound." She saw Tetisheri's expression. "You are surprised. Why?"

"Oh, not by the Mauretanians, or by the fact that war is coming. War is always coming." She hesitated and then came out with it. "I am... grateful for your willingness to share information."

"Because of my reputation for always getting my fee up front?"

"Well... yes."

Calliope smoothed the fabric over her knees again.

Tetisheri realized with a faint sense of shock that the hetaira was nervous. That alone would be enough to put one on alert. Combined with the tension in the air since Tetisheri had first mentioned Cyrene, she resolved to pay strict attention to every word Calliope said and the manner in which she said it.

"As it happens, lady." Calliope smoothed her tunic yet again and spoke to her knees. "You could do me a favor."

"In Cyrene?"

"Yes." Calliope swallowed and looked hard over Tetisheri's right shoulder, as if to meet Tetisheri's eyes would give too much away. "I have another dear friend in Cyrene."

"As I said, one hears how rich you are in friends." Tetisheri's voice was flat and emotionless.

"Yes. She is a member of a Cyrenecian merchant's household." Calliope sighed, and shook her head, at herself, perhaps, at her use of the euphemism. "She is a slave there," she said bluntly. "A Greek, from a small village on Ithaka. Pirates attacked and carried away many of the townsfolk to be sold in the Cyrenecian slave market. A few of the best were gifted to Juba, who picked her out to attend to him personally. When he tired of her, he sold her to the merchant."

Tetisheri had many questions but was afraid to ask any of them for fear they would stem this flow of confidence. Who was this woman? What was she to Calliope? How had Calliope come to hear of her whereabouts? How had an enslaved woman in Cyrene managed to communicate with a free woman of Alexandria?

Most importantly, if Tetisheri was about to be asked what she thought she might be, how high in the merchant's favor did this woman stand? Was she valuable enough in his eyes to be watched? To be guarded? To be chained?

Tetisheri began with the easiest question to ask and to be answered. "What is her name?"

"Urania."

"How long has she been a slave?"

"Almost ten years." Calliope's sigh was nearly a sob. "A lifetime."

"Have you offered a ransom?"

Her question went unanswered for so long she looked up, and saw that Calliope's eyes had filled with tears. "I tried. I failed."

"Why?"

"The man I employed told me she refused to go with him, but I can scarce believe that. There must have been some other reason."

"Or your man lied."

Calliope nodded. "Or the man lied. Although I held back half his price until delivery. He didn't argue that he deserved the full amount."

"Still…" Tetisheri was silent for a moment. "What is it you want, lady?"

Again Calliope smoothed the fabric over her knees. When she spoke her voice was the merest thread of sound. "You have been kind enough to speak of my fame in the city. I must tell you that I myself have heard many tales of the lady Tetisheri as well, niece and partner of Nebenteru the Master Trader."

Tetisheri tried to sound indifferent. "Have you?"

"One tale in particular interested me. I wonder if you will tell me if it is true."

"Perhaps. You can but ask."

The other woman began smoothing her tunic again, became aware of it, and clasped her hands together. Her knuckles were white with strain. "It is whispered in Alexandria that the lady Tetisheri makes a practice of helping female slaves escape."

There was a brief, taut silence.

Tetisheri broke it, taking every care to speak without expression. "Since any such action is universally prohibited by authorities everywhere, I would hope that any friend of mine would immediately contradict such a rumor. A person engaging in depriving the owner of legally acquired property would have every right to have such a malefactor arrested by the Shurta for theft and brought before the courts. If found guilty, they could be fined and imprisoned. In some places their entire estate could be forfeit, along with all property belonging to their family. In others, they could find their right hand struck off." She paused to add weight to what she said next. "They could even be put to death."

"Of course," Calliope said, almost inaudible, "one could

never regard any such rumor as other than suspect in as dear a friend to our good queen, the Lady of the Two Lands, as is the lady Tetisheri."

Calliope's face was turned a little away, her eyes downcast. Tears glittered beneath her thick lashes but did not fall. It was an attitude worthy of Herminia, the greatest actress of her day, and the worst of it—or almost the worst of it—was that Tetisheri knew it.

She drew in a deep, she hoped unobtrusive, breath and expelled it on a long sigh. She was undeniably ten kinds of a fool. "That being understood..."

The rest of the remaining time before departure was consumed in a flurry of packing and a checking-off of multiple lists, interspersed by Uncle Neb bellowing her name from his office, the kitchen, the warehouse, the atrium, wherever he happened to be at the moment he realized they'd forgotten something essential to their expedition that only she could find. Then Keren decreed that they absolutely couldn't travel without a kit filled with salves and bandages in case of disease or injury and repeatedly interrupted Tetisheri with a succession of "What ifs?" The Owls were kept in a constant state of motion between the house, the warehouse, the dock, the Emporeum, the shipyard, and at least once the palace. Late the last evening before they sailed, Babak materialized in the doorway of her bedroom with a sealed scroll. Tetisheri accepted it without comment and stowed it inside her bag. Babak lingered in the doorway. Bast meowed at him and Tetisheri looked up. "Was there something else?"

"We're coming with you," he said. "Agape and me."

"Yes... and?"

"Should we pack our good clothes?"

Tetisheri fastened her bag and stood up, rubbing her lower back. "Yes. We should be prepared for every eventuality."

"Our street clothes, too?" By this he meant the rags she'd found them in, the ones they used when they wanted to pass unobserved. No one noticed the multitude of unwashed urchins clustering on every street corner of Alexandria, begging for coin. If one had noticed, one might have had to do something about them. She had only a dim memory of Cyrene but she had no doubt the same circumstances obtained on their streets.

"Yes."

As if he couldn't help it, a grin split his face. "Yes, lady."

He vanished and she listened for a moment to the sound of his rapid footsteps receding down the hallway. He was so very young, as were all the Owls, young enough to consider everything they did a grand adventure. She wasn't entirely sure she liked the fact that their sovereign knew them by name. The rewards attendant on the queen's favor were always accompanied by an equal or greater amount of risk.

She looked at Bast. The elegant little black cat looked up at her with eyes as blue as her own and gave a chirrup that sounded almost like a chuckle. "Easy for you to say," Tetisheri said.

It was past midnight before she laid herself down to try to snatch a few hours of sleep. It was a futile exercise, as a hundred thoughts jostled for place and she tossed and turned until Bast made her displeasure known in no uncertain terms. After which Tetisheri stared up at the ceiling of her new bedroom, which sat in the back of the house where it opened onto the garden, with its own sitting room attached. The bed was new, too, and all would have been well if only Apollodorus had been occupying his side of it.

She missed him. She missed his expression when she caught him watching her. She missed the deep resonance of his voice. She missed, oh by all the gods in the heavens and the hereafter, how she missed his touch, his hard, callused hands seeking out every curve and line of her body, eliciting levels of response and pleasure that had astonished her as much as it had placed her in his thrall.

She missed having him there to tell her why she was really going to Cyrene. Because he would surely know.

She wondered if he missed her as badly.

She didn't see how he could.

She resented his absence. She resented his willingness to absent himself on behalf of the queen. She resented the queen for having requested his absence on her business.

Toward dawn she might have dozed.

5

December 24, 47 BCE
Cyrene

Apollonia, the port of Cyrene, was one of the oldest ports on the Middle Sea. Its citizens were known to insist that it was in fact the oldest. This assertion was enforced by strength of arms in the local taverns and the streets outside them at the height of tourist season. This was especially true of the Cyrenean Greeks, whose ancestors had founded the city well before, according to them, the torch had been lit for the first Olympic Games. The people of Cyrene had little use for upstart, vulgarian Romans with their endless civil wars. They sniffed at Alexandrians whose city had no history to speak of before Alexander. They rolled their eyes at mention of the Egyptians, who were well known to change gods on a near daily basis, and they shook their heads sadly over the Greeks, who, while granted a grudging gratitude for having founded Cyrene in the first place, were held in ill-concealed contempt for having allowed Rome to roll right over the top of them. The glory that was Greece, indeed.

The fact that they were now a province of Rome, as bequeathed in his will by Ptolemy VIII nearly a century before, and as such subject to Roman laws and Roman taxes, must be endured and deplored, certainly. But they were happy to let King Juba take point on relations with Rome which let the rest of them get on with their lives. Rumors abounded around Juba's court and the people of every nationality who frequented it, such that no right-thinking matron would allow her daughters anywhere near it, but by far the majority of Cyrenecians were willing to turn a blind eye so long as the king left them alone in his turn. Which he had shown himself mostly willing to do, so long as they paid without complaint whatever taxes he levied on them.

The port itself had been carved out of a southwestward-leaning bight, with an inner harbor reached by a canal and an eastern harbor protected by an immense stone mole. On a narrow peninsula between the two stood a lighthouse barely a tenth the size of the Pharos. If one were given to making comparisons.

The *Hapi II* made for the inner harbor and the floating slip for transient parking, where they were met promptly by the inevitable customs agents. Uncle Neb surged forward, hands outstretched, face beaming. "Calvin! Tullus! Well met on the day!"

The professional scowls creasing both men's faces eased into broad grins. "Nebenteru of Alexandria, as I live and breathe! It has been too long since your ugly face darkened our shores!" One of the men thumped Uncle Neb on the back. "By all the gods, Neb! I was beginning to think you'd died on us!"

The second man reached up to flick the teardrop pearl trembling at the point of Neb's neat black beard. "What's this, eh? The latest mode in big city fashion come to shame our provincial shores?"

Neb swatted his hand away and smoothed his beard with a caressing hand. "Touch not the pearl, barbarian. You wouldn't recognize true elegance if it came to you in a vision from Isis herself."

The second man looked over Neb's shoulder and his eyes widened. "And who is this? Not the little Tetisheri! Calvin, can you believe it!"

Calvin peered around Neb's bulk in turn. "Well!" He dug an elbow into Neb's side. "Who knew such a scrawny little runt would turn into such a gorgeous woman!"

"I beg your pardon?" Tetisheri drew herself up in mock outrage. "I was always gorgeous."

"My mistake." And then Calvin picked her up and enfolded her in a not entirely avuncular embrace, after which Tullus took a turn. She was disheveled and laughing when she again regained her feet.

Both men turned to survey the *Hapi II*. "And what have we here, eh, Neb? A new addition to Nebenteru's Luxury Goods and Shipping?"

Neb checked Tullus with an upraised hand. "Sea to Sea Imports, if you please, gentlemen."

There followed an adjournment to the Wandering Sailor, the best tavern on the docks, and drinks all around, courtesy of Neb. By the time he signaled for a refill the two agents had been brought up to date on Neb's affairs and were well enough lubricated to share news of Cyrene, its inhabitants, environs, and, yes, visitors to the city. Before the advent of Alexandria, it had been known as having the best school of art, architecture, history, medicine, and other learned subjects anywhere the Middle Sea touched shore. The school had been founded by Socrates' student Aristippus, whose philosophy boiled down to "If it feels good, do it." Aristippus had tempered that dictum by advocating moderation by moral restraint. Over time something had been lost in the translation and the citizens of Cyrene had taken his original philosophy to heart. By reputation King Juba's court was an exemplar thereof. When stuffy old Roman patricians exclaimed in horror, the Cyrenecians laughed at them openly. The city remained to this day any sailor's favorite port.

The Wandering Sailor was opportunely located on a small rise of ground that gave those seated at tables on a long veranda a view of almost all of the port and the whitewashed buildings that followed the curve of its shoreline. The harbor itself was crowded with hulls, fishing boats, freighters, and more than a few imposing warships at anchor, sails furled, oars shipped.

Neb jerked his chin at them. "And what mighty general has graced Cyrene today, eh?"

Calvin rolled his eyes. "They're getting so thick on the ground, it's hard to keep track. But, yes, Scipio, for one."

"Metellus Scipio? Really? So this is where he ended up."

"All the Pompeiians ended up here after Pharsalus." Tullus scowled and in an unconscious echo of Calliope's words said, "The drums are starting to sound. Again."

Uncle Neb felt that war was a waste of blood and treasure

better spent elsewhere, like improving ports and roads for trade, and he enjoyed saying so out loud and often. The three men plunged into a condemnation of the greed and short-sightedness of all rulers who pitched their citizens into conflict without considering those citizens' actual needs and wants. Like free and uninterrupted trade, to begin with.

Tetisheri let her attention wander to the city.

There was the School of Aristippus, a large, white-columned affair that occupied a tall hill of its own. An immense agora adjoined the port with a public bath taking up one full side of it. Two temples, one dedicated to Serapis and the other to Artemis, jostled for place across the way. Soldiers, sailors, stevedores, slaves, housewives, vendors, and craftsmen ebbed and flowed down the streets and around the buildings like a hive of bees. At this distance they sounded like one, too.

By far and away the preponderance of pedestrians were soldiers, though, native Cyrenecians by their look, most of them attired in new tunics, and displaying all the pride and self-consciousness that comes with being sworn into the king's service. Not one of them looked a day over twelve.

Tetisheri wondered who had the training of them. Some Roman legionnaire seconded from Scipio's forces, no doubt. He was probably more interested in spending his pay than in earning it.

Calvin and Tullus had moved on from war to gossip. Nebenteru had many choice tidbits to share, some of which had to do with Julius Caesar and her royal majesty, Queen Cleopatra.

"Did he acknowledge the child?" This from Calvin, clearly incredulous.

Neb shook his head. "He left before the child was born."

"So he wouldn't have to." Tullus, cynically.

Neb shrugged, not looking at Tetisheri.

"But she named him Little Caesar. Not exactly subtle."

"And Horus," Tullus said. "It's on all the new coins."

All humor faded from Calvin's expression. "They say he's on his way to Africa."

Tullus scowled. "Juba should never have allowed Metellus Scipio within twenty leagues of the Five Cities."

Calvin cast a quick look around but everyone seated nearby was wholly involved in their own conversations. Nevertheless, he gave Tullus a warning glance and lowered his own voice. "I served with him in Gaul. Seventh Legion. He could forgive betrayal the first time. A second time, and—" He jerked a thumb across his neck and drained his cup before refilling it from the pitcher and signaling for more. After all, Neb was buying. "Metellus Scipio has been trying and failing to defeat Caesar at anything for years, in women and in war. I'd say even old Pontifex's generosity should have worn thin by now."

Tullus cleared his throat and changed the subject. "The *Hapi II*? Really, Neb? You couldn't think of anything more imaginative than to name your second ship after your first?"

"Excuse me." Neb, at his most dignified. "Hapi has looked after my business very well these past years—"

"Even during the war?"

Neb nodded. "Even during the war, when merchant traders and shipping companies were being bankrupted in every port on every coast of the Middle Sea—"

"Except for the ones shipping arms," Calvin said.

"—and my philosophy, begging Aristippus' pardon, has always been if it isn't broken, don't try to fix it. The best way to encourage the God of the Nile's continued good regard is to continue to honor him on the prows of all my ships."

Tetisheri smiled. "Also, the names are easier to remember."

Calvin and Tullus laughed. Neb stroked the pearl at the end of his beard and smiled. "And the names are easier to remember."

Lunch arrived, a selection of rolls with sweet and savory fillings and another pitcher of the thin, not quite sour wine produced by Cyrenecian grapes.

Calvin swallowed a roll whole and licked his fingers. "I expect you'll be seeing Timur while you're here."

Neb, as if he hadn't been headed for just this destination in the conversation since he stepped on shore, said easily, "Of course, immediately when I leave you here. What have you seen of him lately?"

Tullus frowned. "To be honest, not much." He glanced at Calvin, who shrugged.

Neb raised his eyebrows. "When was the last time you did see him?"

"Come to think of it, it has been some time since we've had to argue over an export tariff." Tullus waggled his eyebrows at Tetisheri and she smiled dutifully. "When's the last time you saw him, Cal?"

Calvin thought for a moment and snapped his fingers. "I remember—it's when that shipment of arts and crafts commemorating the birth of Caesarion made port. All those images of Isis and Horus on jars and bowls and tunics and amulets. When was that?"

"Oh the gods, of course." Tullus rolled his eyes. "Early November or thereabouts, wasn't it? I'd have to check my records for the exact date."

"As I recall everything went pretty fast."

"I suppose." Tullus sounded grumpy. "I didn't charge near enough of a tariff on that pile of tourist bait."

Neb chuckled. "We have our share on every street corner on the Canopic Way. So you haven't seen Timur in over a month?" The two men shook their heads. "Ah well. I'm sure he's about somewhere. I'll hunt him up this afternoon, see what he has to say for himself. If he isn't spice-hunting in the hinterlands."

Calvin cocked an eyebrow. "Silphium?"

"How did you know?"

"You wouldn't be the first trader in port complaining of the lack."

"Really?"

6

DECEMBER 25
CYRENE

They spent the evening settling in and the following morning Dub and Is went in one direction, Agape and Babak in another, Neb in a third, and Tetisheri was left to her own devices. In this case, her own devices meant her queen's.

Itinerant cabrios clustered at the corner of Kyrenaika and Battos, the first street running the length of the waterfront and the second leading over and around the hills of the city from the docks to the palace. The fifth cabrio she questioned, a grizzled, grumpy man, the set of whose shoulders spoke of extended foot service in some Roman century, claimed to know where Cornelia Metella was housed. It took only four stops to ask the way before he drew up his equally grizzled gelding in front of a small but elegant dwelling. A two-columned marble portico was surrounded by a narrow, well-tended garden of roses of every color. Their perfume was so intense that Tetisheri and the cabrio sneezed simultaneously.

She stepped down from the carriage and turned to hand him his fee. "Will you wait for me? I shouldn't be long."

His nose dripping, he inspected the coins she had deposited in his hand, noticed the additional Egyptian drachma, and was maneuvering his horse and vehicle beneath the shade of a convenient cluster of date palms as Tetisheri mounted the steps to the door.

There was a prompt response to her knock, the door opening to reveal a thin woman with cropped graying hair, dressed in a plain white tunic with a leather cord serving as a belt. She displayed deference but not servility, marking the difference between a servant and a slave.

"The lady Tetisheri, of House Nebenteru of Alexandria, to see the lady Cornelia Metella."

The quality of her attire and above all her assurance convinced the woman to admit her at least as far as the atrium while she went to inquire if her mistress might be at home. The atrium was a pleasant room of frescoed walls and marble floor with a square pool beneath an identical square compluvium admitting a shaft of sunlight. A stream of water tinkled delicately into the pond from a cluster of bronze seashells whose sensuous lines managed to give off an air of prurience.

Roses outside, seashells inside, and the frescoes on the wall featured scenes from the life of the goddess Aphrodite, the goddess stepping ashore on Cyprus, the goddess presiding over the judgement of Paris with Helen dressed only in a strophion, the goddess in bed with Ares, the goddess in bed with Hephaestus. The last two scenes left little to the imagination and Tetisheri was wondering who had built this house and what, exactly, he or she had intended by making these images the first things any visitor saw, when the servant returned. "The mistress will see you, lady. Please follow me."

She followed the woman down a short hall to a small parlor furnished with comfortable chairs arranged around a low table. A lyre made of mahogany polished to a mirror finish sat on a stand in a corner.

"The mistress will be with you shortly. In the meantime, please help yourself to refreshments." She made a gesture at the table and Tetisheri saw that it had been set with a pitcher of chilled juice, two small glasses, and a plate of oatcakes.

The servant vanished again. Tetisheri drifted over to the window, which looked out on the back garden, displaying a continuation of the rose theme. Interspersed between the roses was statuary of not very high craft but explicit in the nature of the acts they were depicting. "Who built this house?" she said, and only realized she'd spoken out loud when she was answered.

"Rather ask what this house was used for before its occupants were summarily evicted so that I might take up residence here."

Tetisheri turned.

Cornelia Metella was tall and slender with dark hair braided back into a heavy knot. Tiny curls that looked natural framed a face of traditional Roman beauty in the most patrician definition of the word. She looked like a statue in the classical style come to life. A high forehead, large dark eyes beneath dark, well-shaped brows, high cheekbones, a long, strong nose that was neither too long nor too strong, a full-lipped mouth opening over white, even teeth, a neck that rivaled a swan's in length and grace. If there was any fault to find it was in the firmness of the chin, indicating strength of character and a determined will. Neither would be a recommendation for your traditional, conservative Roman suitor. Her family wealth and connections would have rendered such considerations unimportant. Hence the two husbands.

So far. Tetisheri wondered if her parents were living or if the lady might at long last have some say in her own future.

For the rest Cornelia Metella was a bit taller than Tetisheri with a figure destined for the dreams of any man who beheld it, whose skin was white, clear, and unlined. She did not look at all like the survivor of two husbands, one of whom fell in battle against Julius Caesar, the other having been beheaded before her very eyes. "Lady Tetisheri of House Nebenteru," she said. Her voice was low and pleasing to the ear. "We have not met."

Tetisheri bowed slightly. "We have not, lady. Thank you for receiving me. I come with a message from the Lady of the Two Lands."

It seemed to her that Cornelia stiffened ever so slightly. "Cleopatra?"

"Indeed." She produced the scroll.

Cornelia stared at it for a moment, her face curiously expressionless, before extending her hand. Tetisheri placed the scroll in it.

"If you will excuse me for a moment."

Tetisheri inclined her head and returned to the window, her back to Cornelia and her gaze, perforce, on the imaginative acts commemorated in marble in the garden. There was a bench, she noticed, in front of each statue. Not so much a bench, on closer examination, as a bed.

Neb would have said the statuary was unmarketable to any but a procurer.

She wondered what Apollodorus would have said, and had to repress a smile.

A voice at her shoulder said, "Yes, to everything you are thinking."

"Which would be what, exactly?"

"That this was a house of pleasure before I dispossessed its previous residents."

Tetisheri turned to look at Cornelia.

Cornelia grimaced. "More truthfully they were dispossessed for me."

"By whom?"

"Juba."

To provide housing for the sister of a powerful Roman patrician who might or might not become a valuable ally, which sister was also a highly regarded and admired matron of Rome would only have been expected of her host. To empty out a whorehouse for her to take up residence in was an obvious and pointed insult. Tetisheri raised an eyebrow.

Cornelia sighed. "The alternative was rooms in Juba's palace. Rooms conveniently placed near his own."

"Ah." Tetisheri was silent for a moment. "Your brother, Scipio, is here as well, I understand."

Cornelia answered the question implicit in Tetisheri's tentative comment in oblique fashion. "He is a guest in Juba's palace."

"And his legions?" If he has any, Tetisheri thought.

"His fourteen legions, every man of whom ought to have known better, are encamped outside Carthage, I believe." She shook her head. "He's lost any hope he had of forgiveness from Gaius."

It took a moment for Tetisheri to recognize the family name for Julius Caesar.

"He's not wrong about that, either. He could have surrendered after Pharsalus and begged for mercy, but he still thinks he can beat Gaius in the field. They've been fighting like dogs over the same bones since we were children. There is no stopping them now and I don't mean to try."

Tetisheri remembered Calvin's words. *I'd say even old Pontifex's generosity should have worn thin by now.* Some trace of unidentifiable feeling in Cornelia's voice did make Tetisheri wonder, albeit fleetingly, if Cornelia had been one of said bones. Cornelia was a beautiful woman, and Caesar had a lifelong reputation for seducing anyone who didn't move out of reach fast enough. Scipio would have seen himself as honor bound by his own class to protect the virtue of his sister. And then she thought of the frescoes and the garden statues. "Then, forgive me, lady, but why are you here? Caesar gave you leave to return to Pompey's estates in Italy. You could be living out your life in ease, not to mention peace." Safely out of reach of Juba and her own idiot brother, she thought but didn't say.

"Don't I know it." The statement came out with a force and bitterness that startled them both. Cornelia drew in a deep breath and released it slowly. "Forgive me, lady. Tempers are short these fraught days and I am no exception."

"Don't I know it." Tetisheri's voice was very dry, and after a moment both women smiled.

Cornelia gestured. "Sit, please. Something to drink?"

They sat across the small ebony table from each other, the legs of which, Tetisheri noticed, were carved in pairs of human figures doing what was usually done in private. She might have recognized one that—no. She shut her mind firmly to thoughts of Apollodorus and accepted a glass of juice. It was tart and cool and refreshing after the dusty and jolting journey from the waterfront. Cyrene streets were not the evenly planed stone of Alexandrian streets.

Cornelia put down her glass and tapped Cleopatra's message. "Do you know what she wrote?"

"No."

Cornelia held it out. Tetisheri hesitated for a moment, and then took it.

There were no words, only a drawing depicting the Eye of Isis. There followed the neat Greek K well known to Tetisheri, next to a sketched sigil of Isis and Horus, Cleopatra's personal seal, also familiar.

"Well." She lowered the papyrus and looked at Cornelia with new eyes.

Cornelia was amused and didn't bother hiding it. "As you say."

Tetisheri allowed the papyrus to curl up again and set it on the low table, where it lurked, it seemed to her, as an asp preparing to strike. It was difficult to find something to say. At last she went with the obvious. "May one ask how you know the queen?"

Cornelia leaned back, very much at her ease. "We met when she was in Rome with her father. She was eleven years old. Even then..." She sighed. "I was younger but I could see she was a force with which to be reckoned. For that matter we all could."

"I remember."

Cornelia looked up. "You go back as far as that?"

"Farther. We were in school together." Along with Aristander, now the head of the Shurta, Alexandria's police force, and a few other useful people. Auletes hadn't been entirely a feckless idiot. For one thing, he'd chosen Cleopatra as his heir, which would have been fine but for the fact that her siblings one and all loathed her and not only because she was their father's chosen one.

Only two of them left now. Philo was marinating in his own stew of hatred on Antirrhodos, to which island in Alexandria's harbor his sister had forcibly moved him, and astutely taken the further precaution of having the shoreline constantly patrolled by men sworn to her service. Her sister, Arsinoë, having chosen the losing side in the last war, was imprisoned in Rome and, fingers crossed, would be executed at the end of Caesar's triumph. If he ever got around to having one.

The absence and quarantine of Cleopatra's last two remaining siblings, respectively, made for a much more peaceful life in Alexandria. At least until one of them got loose to practice the Ptolemies' favorite game of fratricide again.

In the meantime, Cornelia was readjusting her ideas. "So you are her Eye." She hesitated. "May I see it?"

Tetisheri's turn to hesitate, but in the end she pulled out the Eye. A miracle of lapis and mother of pearl and turquoise, the Eye seemed to see all. In the right light it sometimes seemed to move. Always open, ever watchful, merciless. A distillation of the character of Cleopatra VII into a single object.

Cornelia Metella's expression was awed, an emotion one did not often see on a Roman patrician's face. "Thank you."

Tetisheri tucked away chain and pendant.

Cornelia raised an eyebrow, her mask of sophistication firmly back in place. "Blindingly convincing."

"As I believe it was made to be."

"Exquisitely so. There is no mistaking it for what it is."

"No." Tetisheri folded her hands on her knee and looked at the other woman, showing only polite interest. "What is it my queen believes I may do for you?"

Cornelia waved an airy hand. "I don't know." She smiled, and Tetisheri didn't like that smile. "Shall we see how things progress?"

The weight of the Eye at her breast gave Tetisheri the authority, so she exercised it. "My queen wonders if you are here in support of your brother."

The smile vanished. "I am not. I am here in support of Pompey's son, Sextus."

Not "my son," Tetisheri noted. And no mention made of Gnaeus.

Cornelia took a long breath and let it out slowly. "He followed my brother here. As did his brother, Gnaeus." Her lips tightened. "A fool's errand, you will say." She laughed, not at all humorously. "As anyone would say."

"You don't anticipate a victory."

A snort. "My brother has perfected the art of snatching defeat from the jaws of victory, and of running away very fast afterward."

"And Sextus…"

"He's a boy in a man's body, with a head full of dreams of conquest and glory. He is not a fool, for all that, and sees the dysfunction in Rome as well as any. Someone has to rule."

"Just not Caesar." Tetisheri took care to make none of her comments questions, leaving it to Cornelia to answer or not, as she chose.

The other woman's mouth twisted into an expression of acute distaste. "It is difficult at this point to see how anyone else could do any better."

Tetisheri mentally reviewed the list of luminaries whose names graced the headlines of the speaker on the rostrum at the corner of the Street of the Soma and the Canopic Way. Pompey, arguably the last Roman living other than Caesar with any ability, was dead by Philo's hand. Antony was a roistering blowhard, everyone hated Cicero, Lepidus was a cipher, and Cato had ripped out his bowels with his own hands rather than surrender to Caesar. It was obvious to anyone with eyes that Julius Caesar would be the end of the Roman Republic, but it was equally obvious that some political entity, however authoritarian, would survive with him in charge. The legions would follow him anywhere so long as he paid them, and with them at his back the outcome was inevitable.

Everyone in the known world had best start learning Latin.

"I am forced to agree." Tetisheri frowned at her hands. "I have business of my own in Cyrene. It may keep me some days, if not weeks." She raised her eyes to meet Cornelia's with what she hoped was the blandest of expressions. "Our ship is moored at the public dock in the harbor, the

Hapi II. A message sent there will always find me, but do not be alarmed if it takes some time."

Cornelia inclined her head. "I don't anticipate the need to leave in a hurry, lady." She smiled, it seemed with an effort. "But one never knows."

She emerged from the house to find that she would not be Cornelia's last visitor of the day. A blocky man with the muscular build and squared-away posture of the career soldier waited for her to pass through the gate. His courteous nod with politely downcast eyes gave her the opportunity for a quick look at his face, which was as rectangular in shape as his torso. Fair hair clipped to the scalp, stubby eyelashes, stubborn chin, the thick neck that came from years divided between pell training and action in the field, said action remembered in scars from wounds received long ago, including the one marring his right ear. His tunic and cloak were well made of good cloth. The brooch that fastened his cloak was a nondescript bronze circle. He waited for her to step onto the street, eyes still downcast, before passing inside the gate and proceeding up the path to the front door.

She walked quickly to the cabrio and climbed in so she could turn to watch him. The door opened immediately to his knock. He was admitted without question. He was known to the maid, then.

Now what could Fulvio, manservant to one Aurelius Cotta, be doing in Cyrene?

More to the point, was he here on orders from his master, or had he come in Cotta's train?

Aurelius Cotta was Julius Caesar's cousin, shield man, and personal legate to Alexandria. As in Caesar had left him behind, to keep on eye on Queen Cleopatra to report back on what the Lady of the Two Lands was getting up to in Caesar's absence.

And, lest we forget, Tetisheri thought, to serve as a reminder to Cleopatra that she occupied her throne on Caesar's sufferance, no more, no less.

Cotta had been in Memphis in October. She hadn't seen him since and she hadn't felt the lack, but she had to admit—albeit grudgingly—that he did rather have the unnerving habit of ubiquity.

The very last thing she wanted in this endeavor—these endeavors, plural—was to have her shoulder overlooked by someone whose letters went under seal directly to Rome where, she had no doubt, they were always first to be opened.

A movement caught the corner of her eye. She bent to run a finger between a strap on her sandal and her skin, and cast a casual glance around her.

There. Almost hidden in the shrubbery of the house next to Cornelia's. A man in unfamiliar livery, but who had the look of a Numidian about him in his slender build and dark skin.

She straightened the strap and looked up from under her lashes. Yes, there was a second man, dressed much the same, imperfectly concealing himself behind an acacia tree in the house on the other side of Cornelia's.

The driver had slept through all this and she leaned forward to tap him on the shoulder. "Huh? Wazzat? Oh." He wiped his chin on his shoulder and reached for the reins to give them a quick snap, which woke up the gelding, who shook his head and nickered. "Where to now, lady?"

"Back to the docks." They set off with a jolt and Tetisheri leaned back, lost in thought.

Just how free to come and go was Cornelia Metella?

7

I s and Dub pretended to drink their way steadily around
the waterfront, in quest of that one establishment that
catered to centurions, and not the ones with the dew still
wet on their staffs, either. The ones who were getting closest
to retirement were generally freer with their opinions, on
everything from the quality of their legionnaires to the
ability of their commanding officers, or lack thereof, at least
among themselves.

The watering holes on the docks tended mostly toward
sailors and prostitutes, with a seasoning of legionnaires
in their first year seeking adventure in probably the first
seaport they'd been to since taking the oath. They drank a
lot, they drank it fast, and they tended to fall on the nearest
willing female whether or not she had her hand on their
purse, which she always did, with her pimp waiting just

around the corner. Sailors in their turn were worldly wise or pretended to be and were notoriously ready to pick a fight with any legionnaire, the younger and greener the better, regarding it part of their chosen profession to acquaint legionnaires with their inferior station in life.

In the last of these establishments they were not enjoying their drinks when the first mate and three crew members of the *Hapi II* walked in. Both parties ignored each other and Is and Dub left shortly afterward.

"Impressive," Dub said outside.

"How so?"

"They knew to say nothing, to pretend they didn't know us."

"Neb pays them well, not least for keeping his secrets."

"Impressive again."

"What this time?"

"That he pays them at all. That he doesn't use slaves to crew his ships. Most do, including the Roman army."

They both remembered the troop transports with the slaves chained to the oars, shackles they would be free of when they died and not before. "Rome will run out of slaves when the legions no longer exist. Which won't be tomorrow."

"Alas, no."

Is looked quizzical. "It's the turn of the wheel, Dub. There's always someone in charge, and it's always the person with the biggest stick. Yesterday, it was the Egyptians, or the Assyrians, or the Persians."

"If you go far enough east I think it still is the Persians."

"Here, today, it's the Romans. Tomorrow, who knows? Every empire is built on slavery. It's why one invades the other. Bodies to pick your olives and warm your bed and you don't have to pay them one blind sesterce. Recipe for getting rich quick: Be on the winning side of a growing empire."

Is sounded uncustomarily bitter and Dub gave him a curious look. Is grinned, it looked like with an effort. "You do know how close we came?"

Dub stopped and looked Is in the eye, unsmiling. "I do. And I know who I have to thank for that not happening, old man. We all do."

Is waved him on and they walked on in silence for a moment. "I know why you feel the way you do," Dub said finally. "But why Neb? He's Egyptian, through and through. They spent four thousand years building those idiot tombs up and down the Nile. Every last one with slave labor. It's his ancestry. Why doesn't he have slaves?"

Is shook his head. "Neb did have slaves."

"What? When? Not since we've known him."

"Not since he took in Sheri."

"Oh?" Dub walked on, thinking. "Oh."

"She wasn't much more than a child when her mother recalled her from Rome and sold her off. Her husband could treat her however he wanted, and he did." Is's shoulders had tightened up and he shook himself to loosen them. "When she ran to Neb and he offered her the partnership, she told him she'd take it only if he freed his slaves, and not on his deathbed, either."

Dub gave a long, low whistle. "I never knew that."

"It's not something she talks about, or likes having talked about."

"Does the queen know?"

"About what?"

"About Tetisheri being forced into marriage."

"What do you think?"

"Then why didn't she do something?"

"Berenice was busy usurping Auletes' throne at the time. Auletes and Cleopatra were in Rome, or maybe Greece. At any rate not in Alexandria." He paused. "I think the queen disposed of Sheri's mother, though. She hasn't been seen since before the war. It may be the best thing I know of the Lady of the Two Lands."

Dub gave him a quick, sideways glance. Is's expression was unrevealing. Even hundreds of miles to the west, it was never safe to say anything derogatory of Egypt's young queen. She had an uncanny way of getting to hear about it, and a forthright manner in bringing it home to roost when one least expected it.

They continued around the bend of the waterfront, dodging swearing sailors and sweating slaves laboring beneath the overseer's lash, and laden carts rumbling awkwardly on mismatched wooden wheels and, inevitably, soldiers in groups of never fewer than three, making for the nearest sluicery. These establishments Is and Dub were happy to leave behind them—the beer they served would be better poured back into the goat, anyway—and the two men moved inland. They passed the chandlers and fish markets and the slave auction—deserted until the next shipment arrived—and the merchant warehouses and the offices of the lawyers who specialized in maritime law, who made more money than the rest of them put together. Drinking establishments there tended to be more refined, if not actually elegant, with subdued atmospheres redolent of money. The beer was three times the price although it was not noticeably better in quality.

They ambled back around to the east side of the port. They passed the granaries and the theater and a small arena and various other public buildings. The brothels here weren't as numerous as the ones on the south shore and there was no advertising, just curtained windows and a door manned by large, armed guards, most of them Roman and a little grizzled but still fit after their time in the legions. They knew their regular customers on sight and admitted them without question.

A thin film of dust rose into the air and they heard the shouts of an optio bellowing at some poor unfortunate group of milites who were stumbling through a practice march. Dub winced. "How well I remember."

"We're out of it now, is what's important. Let's see if we can find where that optio drinks when he's off duty."

"Or... we could just go ask him." Without waiting for a reply Dub headed off in the direction of the noise. Isidorus shook his head, sighed, and followed.

It was another arena, a small one with only two tiers of seats above the inner stone wall, and what looked to be very small accommodations for gladiators, animals, and slaves. Scaffolding and construction materials indicated that more tiers were planned, but at present the arena floor had been transformed into a military camp, with precisely spaced tents arranged along the back. The front was given over to a parade ground and a training area, upon which most of the encampment's inhabitants appeared to be arrayed. Several groups were sweating heavily in the afternoon sun as they practiced marching in step and endeavored not to tread on the feet of the soldier in front of them. Many failed, which did not go unremarked by the optio in charge. Said optio was roughly the size of Atlas, the exposed parts of his skin showing the history of his life in the legions. It looked to have been long and bloody and served mostly in the front lines.

He would have made three of any of the barefaced boys Juba was calling recruits. They all looked hungry. None of them looked happy. Atlas had them well and truly cowed and they assembled in more or less straight lines as they were called, bumping into each other and casting longing eyes at the cook tent.

Dub sniffed the air and made a face. "What in the name of Ceres is that smell?"

"Supper," Is said. "Poor bastards."

One squad lined up side by side, shield on one arm, wooden sword in hand, practicing the quick thrust. They advanced cautiously against another squad, armed alike with shield and sword, who were practicing defense. Not very well, if the bruised and bleeding knuckles were any indication. Another squad lined up with shields and spears and appeared to be mostly engaged in trying not to trip over the butts of the spears. Their shins bore the signs of their success.

"No shin guards."

"No mercy."

"When was there ever any mercy for fish?"

Fish being the less than affectionate name for raw recruits. Is grunted agreement. It caught the attention of the optio in charge of the practice, who gave them a quick once-over. "Hail and well met, comrades. Pastor here."

"Isidorus. With Caesar in Spain."

"Ilerda?"

Is shook his head. "March, march, march."

Pastor hooked a thumb over his shoulder. "It's what we teach 'em. Or try to." He looked at Dub.

"Dubnorix. Also in Spain."

Pastor raised an eyebrow. He was burly with muscle, and had swarthy skin and thick black hair. "You don't look much older than these useless nitwits."

He had a fine, carrying voice, a job requirement for any practicing optio, and his fish looked around to see who he was yelling at who wasn't them.

Is was shorter than Pastor but of much the same construction, a solid, conscientious build of well-trained muscle and the swaggering assurance that came with it. It belied the graying hair that stood up in thinning curls all over his head (he'd started shaving it and then let it grow again when the girls at Edeva's Tavern had protested) and the knowing grin that curled up into an expression that said he knew what would be fun to do, and wouldn't you like to join him?

Dubnorix, on the other hand, was a tall, slim drink of chilled Falernum with an air so nonchalant it could almost be called languid. He had a head of thick dark hair that made all the girls itch to run their fingers through it and heavy-lidded eyes that made him look half-asleep. He was always rigged out in the latest elegant fashion, which mysteriously never became dirty or disheveled. He looked, in fact, arrogant and entitled, the very picture of the dissolute son of a rich merchant with no purpose in life other than to lavish vast sums upon his offspring, who would lose no time in wasting it in riotous living. So long as it didn't muss his clothes.

That the appearance was assiduously cultivated did not leap readily to one's attention. Of the two of them he was de facto the natural target and Pastor obligingly aimed straight at him. "Shall we show them how it's done?"

Dub smiled. "Why not?" He strolled forward to accept a practice sword, holding it in a relaxed grip. He looked around, one inquiring eyebrow raised. A fish scrambled forward to proffer a lightweight practice shield. Dub thanked him with a charming smile and the boy, all of perhaps twelve years of age, looked dazzled and stumbled back into line. Dub slipped the shield over his left arm and flipped the sword a few times. He turned, facing Pastor, and stood still, waiting. He might have stifled a yawn.

Pastor, a bit miffed, raised his own sword and lunged forward in a classic thrust. If this had been battle and the sword steel instead of wood, the stab might have carried through to Dub's heart.

Or it would have been if Dub had still been there. He wasn't. His shield deflected Pastor's blade with a move that was perilously close to casual. Pastor couldn't hide his look of surprise.

Dub stepped back to fall into a defensive stance and waited. Swords, shields, and pilums lowered all around the practice yard as the fish crowded forward to see how it was done. It wasn't quite the clang of steel on steel but the force of the blows resounded throughout the arena, so that there was no doubt that both men were intent on winning, whatever winning looked like in this case.

Is noted with approval that Dub was keeping it legion standard, nothing flashy, nothing to draw the attention of sponsors in the arena, just cut and parry, being mindful of his balance. Balance was everything in a fight. Is himself had taught Dub that over many long years of practice in various yards between Sicily, Spain, and Africa.

Pastor was no slouch himself, focused, practiced, powerful, his size enough to give the most experienced duelist pause. He didn't make many mistakes, other than the first one, in that he had gravely underestimated his opponent. At some point he realized this, and a slow grin curled one corner of his mouth. He dropped his sword and stood back. "Hah." He was sweating slightly.

Dub relaxed, coming upright, handing the practice weapons to a bashful fish. "Good bout." He wasn't sweating. He wasn't even out of breath.

Pastor's laugh was more of a bellow. "You're better than you look, stranger."

"Thanks," Dub said. "I think." He grinned.

They exchanged grips, and Pastor extended his hand to Is, who took it with a grin of his own. Pastor bellowed, "Dismissed! And if tomorrow morning I find one weapon in the armory that hasn't been cleaned the whole lot of you will spend the next week grinding grain for bread!"

He squinted up at the sky. "It's sundown somewhere. A drink?"

Is clapped him on the back. "Several. I trust you know a place where they don't water the wine?"

Pastor bellowed another laugh. "Know a place? I own a place!"

The place was an open tavern that occupied the front half of a lot facing a quiet side street ten minutes' walk from the arena. On a rise above the surrounding structures, it offered a fine view of the harbor well out of earshot of the voluminous and vociferous business of the port. Potted trees and shrubs were scattered between tables and benches, giving the illusion of a garden. "A garden attended by dryads," Dub said, watching with appreciation as a slender maid with flirtatious eyes brought a tray with a pitcher, glasses, and a plate heaped with deep-fried snacks.

Pastor cuffed his shoulder. "None of that, mind you. Or at least," he added fair-mindedly, "not on the job. What the girls do on their own time is their own business."

"Freedmen?"

Pastor nodded. "And women. Slaves are a pain in the ass, always stealing everything that isn't nailed down and running off the moment your back is turned. I don't know why anybody buys one. Paid a decent wage, freedmen are yours for life."

"So your people don't, er..." Dub gestured to the narrow building that occupied the back half of the lot. The bottom floor was an open-air kitchen and bar, where cooks rolled out dough and cut up meat and chopped vegetables. Above was a walled-in second floor.

"We're not a brothel, my boy. Although there are plenty of them to be found in Cyrene." He winked. "As it happens, I have an interest in one or two of those myself." He laid a finger briefly alongside his nose. "But there are plenty of men who just want a peaceful place for a quiet drink and some decent conversation." He gazed around him with satisfaction. "This is that place."

Is filled cups all around and raised his in a toast toward their host. Dub followed suit. They drank. The wine was young but not harsh and went down well with the crispy pastry. "Well now," Pastor said, appraising them through narrowed eyes. "You have the look of retired legionnaires although he—" a jerk of his head at Dub "—is far too young to have achieved that status."

Is made a circle on a bit of spilled wine with the bottom of his cup. "There you have the right of it, friend, although we did serve for a time."

"A time?"

Is shrugged. "A few years."

"With?"

"Caesar throughout. Britannia. Gaul. And as I said, Hispania, toward the end." Pastor rolled his eyes, and Is laughed. "Yes, again you have the right of it. There was very little glory and even less loot in that last action."

"And far too many mountains," Dub said with a grimace, as if he'd really seen any.

"Which legion?"

"The Seventh."

"Ah. Disbanded, now."

"Yes. I left with it, being of the age." Is nodded at Dub. "He followed me." Pastor raised an inquisitive eyebrow and Is shrugged. "I promised his father I'd look after the kid."

It was the first true thing Is had said since they met Pastor. Dub reached for the pitcher to refill everyone's cups. The two older soldiers fell into reminiscences of marches and battles past that sounded like a tour of all the lesser and greater territories surrounding the Middle Sea, most of which were now Roman provinces, including the one they were taking their leisure in now. From there they moved on to scars, in which competition Pastor won without argument. He flexed his left hand, grimacing, a long, thick scar reaching from wrist to elbow pulling at his skin. "Bibracte. Nearly lost the arm. Decided it was time to get out before I actually did."

"So, you're with Scipio here?" Is's remark was so casual as to be disinterested, although Dub knew Is had been steering the conversation toward this moment since they walked into the arena.

Pastor snorted and spat. "Juba."

It was Is's turn to look politely inquiring. Pastor, nothing loth, cast a cautionary look around to see if anyone was within hearing. He leaned forward and dropped his voice. "Caesar is coming. Did you know?"

Is chuckled. "It must be the worst-kept secret since Zeus banged Persephone. I expect Scipio, from what I know of him, is here in Cyrenaica trying to get Juba to come in with him?"

"For all the good it's doing him."

"Juba's not interested?"

"Juba, as ever, is interested in whatever he can put down to the debit side of his accounts without incurring any expense of his own." Pastor realized his voice had risen and sat back.

"Scipio paying anything?"

"He says we'll have all the loot we want when we defeat Caesar and he takes over in Rome."

Is laughed.

"Yes," Pastor said, "no one is holding their breath. There is dissatisfaction, to put it mildly, in the ranks. Multiple retirements. Even desertions. The ones who stick are in it mostly for the regular meals." He waved a hand. "Why I invested in this tavern."

He drank deeply and with enjoyment, and burped. "I retired after Bibracte, ten, eleven years ago I guess it is now. Cyrene is an attractive place, pretty, good weather, price of property hasn't gone up so high you can't afford a bit of it when you go looking. And while Rome has them by the short and curlies, nobody seems to mind very much." He sounded a little surprised, but then that attitude would be understandable in anyone who had spent decades marching against populations armed and organized against them.

"But you're back in the army now?"

Pastor shrugged. "Juba's drafting every able-bodied male he can lay hands on, inside and outside the cities, to the point that the farmers are screaming about getting the crops in so everyone doesn't starve next winter. He needs someone to train them all, and I'm not the only ex-legionnaire who retired here. He paid a handsome bounty on our services, I will say that for him, and real silver coin, too, not empty promises."

"You at all worried you're going to be on the losing side?"

Pastor didn't even try to deny it. "Scipio has yet to win against Caesar and I don't see that changing. All things being equal, I'd just as soon not be left on the battlefield for my own kind to strip. I won't march unless I'm forced to, and I won't let them put me and my company anywhere near the front line." He thought. "Or anywhere near those fucking elephants."

"Tell me." Is clinked his cup to Pastor's.

"And you?" Pastor eyed Is over his wine. "You don't look hungry enough to re-enlist."

Is let go with a big, booming laugh. "Not hardly!" he said, still laughing. "I've had enough of marching in step, thank you."

"What is your business, then?"

Is shrugged. "Security for a merchant in Alexandria. We guard his trade goods en route and he shares a bit of them with us. It's good work. Not too taxing."

"At sea?"

"At sea, on land. We escorted a caravan to Berenike a while back."

"Berenike?"

"East of Syene, on the coast of the Erythraean Sea." Is grimaced. "Lousy road." He saw Pastor's puzzled expression and elaborated with the more common Latin "Pontus Herculis."

"Ah. Yes, of course." Pastor clearly had as little notion of where Pontus Herculis was as he did of Berenike. "At sea," he said. "From where to where? What ports?"

Is shrugged again. "Well. This one, for starters." He grinned. "But all of them, really. All trade routes begin and end in Alexandria, as you know."

"Rome?"

"Often." Is sighed. "Too often."

"I've never been." Pastor sounded wistful.

"You haven't missed much. Crowded, filthy, there's always some mob protesting about whatever the Senate is up to, and the Senate itself..." He waved a hand in front of his nose as if waving away a noxious stink. "You daren't turn your back for fear you'll get a knife in it, and if you can find a room at an inn without bugs I will yield my shield to you."

Pastor laughed, and stretched, making rather a production out of it. Is let his eyes wander over what was admittedly a fine torso. "I'm for the baths."

"Do you know of a good place?"

Pastor brightened. "I do, and not too far from here."

Dub recognized the signs and before Pastor did the polite thing and invited him along he pushed back from the table and stood. "I think I'll ask that nice young woman who brought us our meal what time she gets off work."

Is winked at him and followed Pastor out into the street.

8

Neb had secured a generous suite of rooms at the
Waterfront Inn, a clean, commodious establishment with a good kitchen and a decent cellar. Four
comfortably furnished bedrooms were arranged around
a central parlor with doors opening onto a balcony. The
Hapi II was moored almost directly across from it. Neb
could and did wave at Jerome, the ship's captain, who could
be seen scurrying nose down from bow to stern, hunting
out any defects in his new darling. The fact that he was
constantly in motion indicated he wasn't finding any, which
pleased Neb greatly.

They'd had a generous following wind from Alexandria
and had taken the journey slowly, running the new ship
through her paces, stopping at various small villages with
piers large enough to accommodate the new ship. Jerome had
brought the oarsmen through every beat and combination

of beats in their repertoire, until down to the youngest seaman they were confident in their ability to warp into any dockside without breaking an oar or scraping the paint, and at sea to put on enough speed to discourage any pirate. In case speed was not enough, they regularly practiced repelling boarders with bows and arrows and the small ballista that hurled short, barbed spears with devastating accuracy, so much so that just bringing them out on deck was often enough incentive for pirates to change course.

They had trimmed the large, square sail to accommodate every possible change of wind, to the point that the trail of a horned viper through desert sand was nothing compared to their wake. The crew had taken it in shifts to examine the caulking of every joint and seam once they got underway, as well as the splice of every line and the craft of every knot. Amphorae were filled with sea water and placed in their cradles in the hold, and emptied again once Neb was satisfied that none of them were going to be shaken loose in a heavy sea to beat the *Hapi II* to pieces from the inside. The cargo nets were loaded to the maximum one at a time—once with members of the crew, so as to test the load-bearing capabilities of the winch and the boom—and inspected for stretching and fraying afterward.

By the time the last line was made fast in Cyrene (and they had not made fools of themselves before the hundreds of interested eyes upon them in so doing), Neb was willing to admit himself satisfied. Upon their return to Alexandria Demetrius would get a bonus and the go-ahead to lay the keel for the *Hapi III*.

Breaking their fast the next morning, Neb looked preoccupied and not a little worried. "I went to the warehouse where we rent space. They haven't seen Timur in more than a month and they are tired, they tell me, of answering the door to creditors clamoring for payment."

"Did they open our offices and storage for you?"

"They did."

"And?"

He shook his head. "There is very little there. Some dried herbs that crumble at a touch—no, no silphium—and..." He shrugged. "A small collection of scrolls, nothing that looked very exciting to me, but I gave them to Jerome for transport back to the Library."

Tetisheri smiled. "Currying favor with our queen?"

"Always," he said dryly.

"Any sign of Timur's books?"

"No." He sighed. "He never invited me to his home, so I don't know where he lives."

"Tullus and Calvin?"

He tugged at his pearl. "Evidently Timur belonged to some obscure Zoroastrian sect that keep their women in seclusion. Tullus and Cal never saw his home, either, but they did say he spoke of it as being on the outskirts of the city, and that he always arrived in one of the public cabrios. I'm going to inquire among them today." He paused. "The office was empty, true, but it showed no signs of a hurried departure."

"Ah." Tetisheri frowned. "Well, that means he's probably still alive."

"One hopes."

"We'll find him, Uncle."

"I don't know that I want to," he said heavily.

Tetisheri wasn't sure she wanted to, either. Alive was one

problem, a factor who had perhaps absconded with company funds, a man esteemed by both Neb and Tetisheri who had given perfect satisfaction since before the Alexandrian War began.

Dead, well, dead raised a host of other problems, not least of which was who had killed him, and why, and if it had anything to do with his employment.

"And the silphium?"

A thunderous oath. "Would you believe it? It is just as Tully and Cal said! None to be had the length and breadth of the docks!"

Tetisheri shook her head, puzzled. "Has someone cornered the market? Bought it all up and has it stored somewhere?"

"But why? When they could name their own price?" Neb threw up his hands. "They always could have!"

Her uncle looked so disheartened that Tetisheri's heart melted. "And how are plans for the party coming?"

His countenance lightened, but he said, "What party?"

She chuckled. "Don't be coy, Uncle. I don't imagine we're carrying all those trade goods in the *Hapi II*'s hold back to Alexandria with us."

He might have preened, just a little, before capitulating. "In two days' time. I have secured the common room on the floor below."

She nodded encouragingly. "A large, well-aired room filled with light. A good choice."

"The size is no matter," he said with an airy wave. "It will be a small, select group."

From long experience Tetisheri knew what that meant. She could be confident of seeing most of the Cyrene merchant class present, some in attendance on those noble patrons who funded their purchases, possibly up to and including the king, although she sincerely hoped it would not.

Fortunately Neb, whatever "small" and "select" protestations he made, knew that, too, and she could be sure he would lay in enough refreshments so that no one would go away hungry or thirsty. He went off to consult with the landlord and she peeped into the room that served as a temporary mews for her Owls, where two small mounds of blankets were beginning to stir. She closed the door softly and went to order tea and more breakfast. It had arrived by the time they emerged, yawning, but with clothes in good order and hair groomed.

"About time, too." Tetisheri nodded at the table and the two sat down and loaded their plates. Their days on the streets of Alexandria were behind them but they had learned survival in a hard school and they never passed up a meal. While their attention was so fixed Tetisheri checked Is and Dub's room. Empty, and their beds hadn't been slept in.

She refilled her cup and sat down again. "Have you had enough, or should I send for more?"

She wasn't joking and they'd worked for her long enough to know it. Babak grinned, a white slash in his dark face, black eyes merry. He was attired in a tunic that had somehow survived the voyage unwrinkled, and sported the badge of House Nebenteru, as did Agape, although she somehow contrived to made her tunic look made to measure, which it most certainly wasn't.

Tetisheri made a mental note to make tactful inquiries

into the girl's background. She was curious, true, but that knowledge would go a long way toward tailoring Agape's future duties. If she could pass herself off as the child of a wealthy or even a noble house, she would be worth her weight in gold.

Agape nipped the last piece of bread from beneath Babak's hand. She had neater table manners but she packed away every bit as much food as he did and made sure she got her share, too.

Tetisheri sipped her tea and set down her cup. "Report."

Unconsciously both straightened in their chairs, shoulders back, hands folded, expressions professionally serious as befit retainers of those in service to the Queen of Alexandria and Egypt.

"The house was easy to find," Babak said. "It's one of the largest in the city, second only, some say, to the royal palace. Its owner is one of the city's richest men, at least by repute."

"What makes him rich?"

"He owns many farmlands to the south of the city."

"Inherited?"

Babak shook his head. "He is a favorite of Juba."

"Why?"

"He supplies arms to Juba's army. Juba repays him in property."

"Convenient. Were you able to get into the house?"

Agape looked disdainful. "Two guards only, both on the front door."

"And?"

At Tetisheri's tone Agape moderated her attitude. "I went around to the kitchen with a list of the herbs Uncle Neb brought and bespoke the cook."

Tetisheri noticed the unconscious use of the familiar title and hid a smile. Agape might try to hold herself aloof but not even she was proof against Uncle Neb's charm.

"Titrit, the cook, recognized my badge immediately. She had me read her the list and started making out an order." She looked at Babak.

"While she was distracted I snooped around the kitchen. They were busy, getting ready for the party."

"Party?"

"Laurus is holding an open house this evening in honor of Saturnalia. All of Cyrene will be there, or all of those who matter." He saw Tetisheri's eyebrow rise and grinned. "I'm quoting, lady. I fell into conversation with the slave making the cakes and rolls. She is beautiful." His voice was reverent. "Greek, I think. Slim, brown hair with golden lights all through, beautiful skin." He grimaced. "Other than her hands. From the scars and calluses I'd say she's been working in the kitchen for a while. Still, I don't know what she's doing in the kitchen when she could be taking her ease in the master's bed." He scratched his head. "She reminded me of someone but I can't think who."

"What was she doing?"

"She was making rolls and cakes." He smacked his lips. "She let me taste a few. They were very good. One of them was nuts ground with honey between layers of crust rolled so thin the light shone through them. I'm going to ask Phoebe if she can make some." He paused. "She was kind. She didn't have to be. The good will of someone else's servant wouldn't earn her anything. But she was." He sighed. "And so very beautiful."

Agape rolled her eyes. "I talked a bit to Titrit and admired how big her kitchen was and how many slaves she had working for her. She's a freedwoman herself."

"Unusual," Babak said.

"How so?"

"I got to talking to one of the pages, Idir his name was. He said Laurus never allows his slaves to work their way to freedman."

"How did Titrit come to work for him?"

"Idir said Laurus hired her away from Titrit's previous employer after enjoying a dinner he had attended there. But Idir says that Titrit is the only freedwoman he has in his employ."

"What does Titrit say of her employer?"

"Nothing good. Nothing bad, either."

Babak shrugged. "Not surprising. One word of criticism that gets back to the master and Titrit could be beaten for slandering his good name. Idir says Laurus doesn't spare the whip. Whipped, or cast forth with no recommendation for future employment."

Agape shook her head. "I don't think so, lady, or at least not cast forth. We saw Laurus climbing into his house cabrio as we were leaving. The springs barely held him up off the ground."

Babak snickered. "Agape has the right of it, lady. Laurus has the look of a man who enjoys his food above all else. It's no wonder he keeps a prize like Urania in his kitchen instead of his bed."

"Urania?"

"The baker. The Greek slave."

"Ah."

Uncle Neb bustled back in, full of plans for his party. He

knew of Laurus and nothing to his credit. "Laurus! That fat old sword smuggler! Do you know, he once hired the *Hapi* to ship a load of grain from Cyrene to Cyprus? Said it was a new strain, more nutritious, it ground finer flour, the bread made from it rose as high as Olympus." He gave a loud and indignant snort, the pearl at the tip of his beard quivering with outrage. "My eye. Buried inside every sack of grain were enough arms taken all together to outfit a legion, which I make no doubt is what Arsinoë and Philo had planned to do with it!" He humphed again. "He's hosting a Saturnalia party, you say?" He snapped his fingers. "Hah!"

Which meant there would be no comparison between Laurus' party and his own. Tetisheri feared the event had just doubled in price.

"We should go," she said in a voice as indifferent as she could make it.

Neb was arrested in mid-tantrum. "To Laurus' party?"

"Yes."

"Without invitation?"

She looked at him from beneath her lashes. "I'm sure we didn't receive one only because Laurus didn't know we were in town."

Neb snorted again, but with less force this time. He was considering it, no doubt planning to take mental notes so as to outdo Laurus at every turn. He turned a shrewd eye on his niece. "Why?"

She thought of Fulvio disappearing into the brothel Juba had appropriated for Cornelia Metella's benefit. "I think it might be... educational."

Neb gave her a very old-fashioned look, which said he knew perfectly well for whom she would be educating herself at this gathering of prominent and powerful Cyrenecians. "Well, my dear, I'm afraid Laurus would not look kindly upon me as a guest in his house—I did turn him in to the authorities over that arms affair, after all—but you may go, if you really wish to." He held up one admonitory finger. "Not unattended, however. Both Isidorus and Dubnorix will escort you."

"Certainly, Uncle." She turned to find the two Owls regarding her expectantly. "You brought your best clothes?"

They nodded.

"Good. Pull them out and make sure they will reflect well on your employer."

They brightened. "We're going to the party, too?"

"You are."

Agape and Babak disappeared into their room. Tetisheri went to the window to look out on the harbor.

Cleopatra wanted confirmation that Juba really was siding with Metellus Scipio in the coming fight against Caesar.

Caesar... well, it was no secret that Caesar wanted everything he could get, by any means necessary. If Tetisheri's little mission, or missions, here in Cyrene could aid him in that endeavor, he certainly wouldn't turn said aid down.

And if one of Cleopatra's own was responsible for giving Caesar any advantage, she would be happy to take credit for it.

Cornelia Metella wanted to extract Sextus from Scipio's influence. Possibly Gnaeus, too.

And then there was Calliope's plea, no, no, let's not forget that.

Neb wanted to find Timur.

So did she.

They both wanted to find a marketable quantity of silphium, although finding Timur in good health, preferably without a guilty conscience, took precedence. A worthy goal, but possibly an unrealistic one. People didn't just disappear, but if disappearing was their idea in the first place...

She had no standing here in Cyrene, other than as Neb's partner. The Eye of Isis amulet seemed to warm on her breast as she thought of it, but it carried little to no weight here in Cyrenaica, except perhaps for any Egyptians or Alexandrians resident in the city. She wasn't the queen's official envoy to Juba's court because that would demonstrate too formal a relationship between two countries who had been at sword's point since Juba had come to the throne. Cyrenaica had been under Roman rule for fifty years and joined to Crete as a senatorial province for nearly twenty. Dying rulers kept leaving their kingdoms to Rome in their wills. Auletes had. Twice. It was something of a miracle that Cleopatra still occupied her throne more or less independently, although that had more to do with no Roman senator being willing to cede to any other, and most especially not to Caesar, the financial advantage of governing the wealthiest property on the Middle Sea.

Caesar's libido, too, that had unquestionably been a factor.

So Tetisheri wasn't an envoy, or an emissary, or an

ambassador. She was only a humble merchant, who had to buy her way into favor like any other merchant. Neb's party might go some way toward accumulating favor. There might be something useful to be learned at Laurus' Saturnalia celebration, too, depending on the guest list.

She thought again of Fulvio at Cornelia Metella's house. If Aurelius Cotta was here, he was here to report to Caesar. She thought back to her conversation with Calliope. *There are many Romans resident in Juba's court at present.* But Cotta was as well known as his cousin, as was his allegiance to that cousin. He'd come here on the quiet, too, although Cleopatra must have known that he'd left Alexandria because Cleopatra always knew everything.

She wondered if Cotta's presence in Cyrene was the reason for her own. She wondered if Cotta had come face to face yet with Metellus Scipio. Or Juba. On the whole she thought not or the reverberations would have been felt from Cyrenaica to Bocchus' court in Mauretania in the west, to Cleopatra's in Alexandria in the east.

She wondered what would happen if and when he did. She would have paid good money for a seat to that performance. Because it would have been a performance, meant to be conducted in front of witnesses who would have been all too pleased to forward their first-hand accounts to Caesar.

Below her the wharves of Cyrene extended out in graceful curves to the left and to the right. Up the hills in back of the harbor a jumble of tile roofs jostled for place with acacia and tamarisk trees, full-blown canopies providing some defense from the heat and glare of the noonday sun. Before her the port swarmed with activity, longshoremen and sailors, soldiers and slaves, fishermen, housewives, and merchants and lawyers, all preoccupied with their own concerns. She wondered how many of those concerns had anything to do with the forces of war massing on their horizon.

It was a beautiful city, as cities founded by Greeks usually were. Seven hundred years before, emigrants from the island of Thera arrived here, bringing their white columns and carved friezes, along with all the gods in their pantheon, and their love and mastery of the sea. No Middle Sea harbor had been safe from the Greeks, and this was a nice one.

Across the way, the *Hapi II* bobbed at its moorage. Evidently Neb had already done a bit of shopping because the crew was taking on cargo from a laden cart drawn up to the edge of the dock.

The door opened behind her and she turned to see Dub and Is enter. "And where have you two been, and what have you been up to?" she said in mock reproof.

Is's grin made him look even more satyric than he ordinarily did. Dub raised an eyebrow back at her and refused the bait.

"Food?"

"I could eat," Dub said, and Is nodded. Tetisheri nodded at Babak, who had poked his head out of their room. He vanished through the door and they could hear him taking the stairs two at a time.

"Well?" Tetisheri sat down. "Did you take the pulse of the city?"

"You could say that." They waited until Babak returned with a tray of fruit, cheese, boiled eggs, and meat rolls and a pitcher of small beer. They filled plates and cups and fell to.

"So? What's the news? And who did you hear it from?"

Is mopped up the last of the oil from his plate with a scrap of bread and popped it in his mouth. "Well," he said thickly, "neither Juba nor Scipio's legions have a lot of faith in their ability to pay them." He drained his cup and refilled it and Dub's. "Mostly because they haven't yet."

"They're barely feeding them as it is," Dub said. "I've never seen fish with less flesh on them."

Is nodded. "And both regular armies are unhappy about the current conscription policies. Basically, Juba is snatching up every able-bodied male—"

"—the definition of 'able-bodied' including males aged ten and up—"

"—and putting them under arms whether or not they know how to use any weapon more offensive than a hoe."

"And most of them don't."

Tetisheri nodded. "So… they're broke and hungry."

"To the point that some of them are seeking, ah, alternative sources of revenue."

"Really. Such as?"

"Taverns, brothels, rental property, import and export." He and Is exchanged a glance. "But what's the most profitable trade there is?"

Is nodded. "And it's not even illegal."

"The slave trade." The words came out flat and unemotional, although Tetisheri felt anything but.

"I met a girl last night—"

"You always meet a girl," Is and Tetisheri said in unison, and Babak snickered.

"—a friendly little Greek girl. She has a room in a boarding house not too far from where she works—" he nodded at Is "—also owned by Pastor—"

"Pastor?"

"I'll explain in a minute. Or Is will." He winked at Is. "Anyway, nice room in a respectable-looking house in what appears to be a good neighborhood, and, remarkably, she's not sharing it."

"She must make a good wage."

"You would think. But she says Pastor says he keeps the rents low to subsidize housing for his employees. Of which he apparently has more than a few because all the rooms in this house are full, and all the residents are his employees. There's a hostess on staff who cleans, and cooks, too, if you pay for it, and who collects the rent. If you miss a week, Sappho—"

Is choked over his cup.

"—shut up, Is—Sappho says they won't demand interest when you catch up."

"Anyone's dream landlord."

"Indeed. Additionally, Sappho has more than one tunic, some stolas, scarves, at least two spare pairs of sandals, all of good quality."

"A propertied young lady, indeed. Where does she work, again?"

"Server in Pastor's taverna."

Tetisheri was quiet for a moment. "Does she have family?"

"If she did she'd be living at home, now, wouldn't she?"

"Is she local?"

He nodded. "So she says. She has some small mementoes, too, she says gifts Pastor or his friends bring back from their travels."

Slaves didn't have mementoes. Slaves were lucky to have a tunic to stand up in. "'Their travels?'"

Dub nodded. "Pastor and his friends disappear from time to time, return in a week or ten days."

They thought this over. At the end of the table Babak and Agape remained quiet and still, hoping no one would notice they were still there and order them from the room.

Tetisheri sat back and looked at Is, letting the silence in the room gather.

He felt her gaze without looking up from the fascinating contents of his cup and grimaced. "Everything Dub said, and one thing more." He met her eyes, his expression rueful. "Pastor knows Timur."

He watched Tetisheri's eyebrows go up and nodded. "I think they're in business together."

9

Neb had a trying afternoon that wore appreciably on his normally sunny disposition. Cyrene's cabrios one and all were determined to take him for a ride, literally as well as metaphorically. Not a one was able to find Timur's home but they were happy to try to find it on his drachmae, and the longer it took the better, for their purses if not for his.

Someone must have pinned the word "chump" to his back in Latin, Greek, and Numidian. A glum thought and one that stung his pride. Further, the sun was descending inexorably into the west and he had no faith in his current driver's ability to find his way back to the docks in the dark. "See here," he said abruptly to the back of the man holding the reins of an old, cranky roan, "if Timur's house isn't found in the next ten minutes, you may return me to the inn."

"Certainly, sir, of course, sir, whatever you say." The driver pulled on the reins and brought the recalcitrant roan around in a neat, three-point turn. At the next intersection they turned right without hesitation and proceeded south and uphill. At the top of the hill they turned right again along a well-maintained dirt road carved from the face of the hill. Due to the hill's steep gradient the houses built on both sides had an unobstructed view of the city all the way to the port and the deep blue expanse of the Middle Sea beyond. Neb squinted and imagined that he could see the *Hapi II* at her moorage.

The houses were large and handsome, set back from the edge of the road and landscaped with trees and flowering shrubs. It was a very nice neighborhood, almost Alexandrian in style and quality.

The cabrio drew up. "This might be Timur's house, sir."

But Neb had already seen the insignia over the front door. He got out and looked at the hand that the cabrio had extended beneath his nose. "I'll pay you when I'm safely back at the Waterfront Inn."

The roan jumped and sidestepped and tossed his head, possibly beneath an incautious hand on the reins. "It's coming on dark, sir."

"Is it?" Neb said cordially. "I hadn't noticed." His voice hardened. "If you want to be paid, you'll wait."

Honor satisfied, he turned to descend the steps to the front door, ignoring the grumble behind him.

No one answered when he knocked, nor when he thumped so loudly that even he could hear the sound echoing inside. He looked up and saw that the cabrio was still there. The shape of the driver's shoulders looked resentful. Too bad.

There was a path around the house between two orderly rows of well-manicured shrubbery. He followed it, coming eventually to another door situated behind an open-air kitchen very much like his own, but faced with more expensive tile in an attractive blue floral pattern.

He had no time for either admiration or envy, however. He knocked again, and again there was no response. He looked around the yard beyond the kitchen. Unlike Alexandria, Cyrene didn't have running water or indoor plumbing so the well and the necessary were expected, although they were a little too close together in his opinion, and far too close to the kitchen in anyone else's. The garden here, being out of sight of the street, was less formal, including a kitchen garden behind a fence. Another fenced area encompassing swings and toys formed a well-used playground.

This time he thumped on the door. Once only, because it unlatched beneath the force of the blow.

He stood looking at it for a moment, at the darkness that lay beyond it. "Hello? Timur? It's Neb. Are you there?"

There was no response. For no reason he could think of, a shudder ran down his spine and he nearly quit the place then and there.

What would Tetisheri do? Would his intrepid niece, who had survived far worse than a dark and empty house, would she have turned her back and walked away?

No, she would not.

He went to the kitchen and found a small oil lamp. A handful of dead weeds made a spill which kindled at the first strike of the firesteel he always carried at his belt. The wick was nearly dried out but lit with a little coaxing. He waited for the flame to steady, and carried it to the door. Holding the lamp high in one hand, he pushed the door all the way open with the other.

And then immediately jumped back when some small rodent shot out between his feet and buried itself in the shrubbery. He recovered his balance, waited for his heartbeat to steady, and went in. He would never admit his momentary fright to a soul, or even to himself.

The twilight outside deepened on the inside. He appeared to be in a combination pantry and scullery, with a long table down the center of the room, a sink and cupboards around the walls. Every cupboard door stood open. It appeared as though everything in them and on the various shelves had been pulled out and let fall haphazardly to the floor. He went around the table, broken shards of pottery crunching beneath his feet. He accidentally kicked a small metal pitcher that impacted the table leg with a resounding bang and went tumbling out of sight. Grain, flour, dried fruits, spices, all had been upended over the floor and their containers broken.

So.

A door in the center of the opposite wall beckoned, on the other side of which he found a hallway that appeared to run the length of the house. He glanced through other doorways and found the same disarray, chests and containers broken open, clothes, cosmetics, scrolls, household goods strewn across the floor.

He paused for a moment, thinking. The search had been thorough, and, he felt, professional. This wasn't just a message. The searchers had been looking for something, something specific, and all containers of every size had been searched, which probably meant something small. Wall hangings and two fixed wardrobes had been pulled free of the walls, holes made in the walls behind them, vases and bowls and chests broken and overturned, the mattresses of five beds cut open with the stuffing removed and pulled apart so that the floors of the bedrooms were covered in white drifts of cotton.

He stood for a moment, thinking. It was a deliberate mess, yes, but less of a mess than he would have imagined there would be with three wives and however many children in residence. He imagined what his home, old or new, would have looked like following the same treatment, and shuddered. They would be weeks if not months sorting it out and setting it to rights again.

A very small peristylium sporting two columns only led him toward a source of dim light, which proved to be the atrium. The opening in the roof allowed what was left of the day's light to illuminate, if only dimly, the interior. An oval pool occupied the center of the room. Inside, there was water. No fountain.

He saw him when he looked up, or rather a shadow of someone sitting in a corner. "Timur?" There was no answer. "Timur, it's Neb. Nebenteru of Alexandria." Again, nothing.

He knew then, but something in him refused to acknowledge it in so many words. He forced himself to walk around the pool and approach the figure. "Timur?"

He held up the lamp. The flame flickered in the slight breeze coming down through the compluvium but the wavering light was more than enough to see. He stumbled back in horror, tripped over the edge of the pool, caught his balance and splashed out the other side, wet to the knee, where his toe caught on something solid but giving. He pitched forward onto his hands and knees and found himself face to face with an unknown man, more recently dead than the man in the chair, eyes staring sightless at the ceiling.

He was frozen in place for a time that could have been a moment or the whole night, before he managed to push himself to his feet and feel around for the dropped lamp. Most of the oil had spilled out of it and he went back down the hallway and out into the kitchen to find another. This one was harder to light, probably because his hands were shaking. When the flame caught and steadied, he stared into it for a moment, taking what comfort he could from the tiny, golden warmth. It was cold in the house and he was chilled to the bone.

Although that might not have been solely due to the lack of a fire.

Resolute, he picked up the lamp and forced himself to return inside, walking slowly but steadily back to the atrium. Swallowing hard, he went first to the man in the chair, who had been bound to it and left there as they had worked on him. His face was unrecognizable, but they had left the amulet around his neck on its brown cord. The Lion of Samarkand, the same image that had been set into the lintel over the front door. This lion was carved from the golden oak of Punt and polished to a gleaming shine. Timur's people had come from Sogdia, and Neb had never seen Timur without that emblem of his ancestry.

His fingers, all of them, had been broken, the nails of each one ripped off. His elbows and knees were misshapen, so very likely they had been broken, too. His feet— Nebenteru looked away. The rodent who had dashed out of the back door had been feeding on them.

Whatever Timur had done, even if he had embezzled from all of his clients, including Neb himself, no one deserved this treatment. No one deserved this kind of death.

Timur's body was almost desiccated. He longed for the presence of Keren, who never turned a hair in these situations and who could have told him chapter and verse what had happened here and when, coolly and with precision. But while he was no such expert, he could tell Timur had been here for a long time. More than a month, perhaps. When had Neb last heard from him? His thoughts felt frozen in place.

He would have closed Timur's eyes, if Timur had had any left. He cleared his throat. "I hope Anubis prepared the way for you, Timur, and Osiris welcomed you into the Duat. Be at peace now, friend."

He bowed his head for a moment.

Then, as one honor bound to complete the task, he stiffened his spine and turned to examine the other body.

Even in the wavering light of the lamp it was obvious that this was a fresh kill, this morning, perhaps last night. The flesh was cold, the limbs stiff. It had not yet begun to smell. Keren, probably even Tetisheri, would be able to assign a time of death if they were here, but they weren't. He steeled himself and bent to search the body. A purse, emptied, of course. The clothes were serviceable but well worn, his sandals good leather but, again, nothing stylish or expensive. There was a bloodstain on his tunic below his left breast. Even Neb could see the result of a single thrust, under the rib cage straight into the heart.

The sign of someone who knew what he was doing.

Neb stood up, frowning, holding the lamp so as to direct its light toward the man's face. He looked familiar but Neb could not immediately put a name to him. He noted his features, the fair hair clipped short, the broken nose, the right ear that had been partially torn off and sewn back on, the callouses on his hands, the scars on his knuckles. His arms and calves were heavily muscled and together with the set of his shoulders all but shouted "Soldier!" Any doubt of that conclusion was put paid to by the sword, a well-used and well-cared-for standard issue gladius, lying just out of reach, looking as if it had fallen from his out-flung hand. Disarmed, it looked like, just before the killing blow thrust through his heart.

He had seen all he could, and there was nothing he could do now but leave this place.

He almost blundered out the front door in his haste to be gone but caught himself in time, leaving it locked and barred as he'd found it and exiting the house the same way he'd come in.

Miracle of miracles, the cabrio was waiting for him, possibly because the driver had fallen asleep over the reins. He climbed in and was surprised at how steady his voice was when he said, "Back to the Waterfront Inn, driver, if you please."

The driver woke up with a mumbled, "Certainly, sir." He smacked the reins against the roan's back to wake up the horse, too. With a jerk and a shudder they were off.

It was well past sunset when they turned onto the street that fronted the docks. As they pulled up in front of the inn, for the first time Neb realized he was still holding the lamp.

10

They were late to Laurus' house, but as Dub pointed out they weren't invited so it didn't really matter what time they arrived. There was a large quantity of vehicles parked up and down the street, ranging from the common cabrio to chariots with the spokes of their wheels picked out in gold. They parked a few streets away, well out of sight, and proceeded on foot.

Their driver chuckled beneath his breath when they asked him to wait. "You sure you don't want me to come back in the morning?"

Tetisheri looked at him in surprise. "Quite sure. You won't lose anything by it, I assure you."

This time he laughed. "Ah well, you can always change your mind."

He was still laughing as they walked away.

"What was all that about?"

"It sounds like he knows a bit more about this party than we do." Is loosened his blade in its sheath. Dub did the same almost in unison. Agape and Babak exchanged a wide-eyed glance and drew closer together, and closer to Is and Dub while they were at it.

When they arrived at the portico of Laurus' home the doors stood wide, lacking any attendant.

Is sniffed. "Lousy security."

"All the better," Dub said.

Tetisheri inspected her company. Is and Dub wore House Nebenteru livery, Agape and Babak their best tunics with House Nebenteru brooches pinned to their left shoulders. She herself wore a tunic of heavy silk dyed blue to match her eyes, under a palla of lighter blue fastened with a finely worked bronze pin in the shape of a ship in full sail. She didn't have the patience to tie her thick black hair back into a coronet of fifty tiny braids in the current fashion and had instead smoothed it into an unwieldy knot at the nape of her neck. How long it stayed there was another matter.

"Remind me again why we're here?" Is looked even more like a bad-tempered satyr than usual.

"We are told everyone in Cyrene comes to Laurus' gatherings. We ought to be able to find some interesting conversations to listen in on. Be discreet."

Everyone looked offended and with a roll of her eyes she led the way inside, there to gather any available information that might be valuable to her uncle, her business, and her queen.

The gathering was being held, as customary, in the largest room in the house, the atrium, which Laurus had filled with couches and benches surrounding the impluvium. Centered in the impluvium was a plinth, upon which stood a round, shallow bowl glazed so deep a red it appeared to be bleeding. Slaves in red tunics passed large trays and pitchers, and there was a hum of conversation and muted laughter. It stilled when she appeared as all eyes turned to her. She knew an instantaneous, uncomfortable feeling that she had been stripped down to her skin.

A thin man twice Tetisheri's age, with his remaining hair in a Caesar combover, tripped over his sandals on his way to leer directly into the front of her tunic. "Ah, shomeone new to join ush, eh?" He reached out an unsteady hand and flipped her amulet up. "I'll be sure to look for the 'ittle—little back catch when the time comesh."

Dub stepped up smartly and smacked the drunk's hand away before it could settle somewhere on Tetisheri's person.

"Be off with you now, sir."

"Shfine. I can wait." He staggered off, falling onto a couch occupied by two matrons who, far from taking offense, fell into gales of inebriated laughter.

There was a lot of laughter coming from every direction, loud and raucous. Everywhere Tetisheri looked some man was watching her with an appraising expression. There was an air of, she could only call it anticipation, permeating the atmosphere, taut, expectant, and barely leashed. She felt as if she was in the presence of a room full of predators, and on the wrong side of the bars at that.

She had encountered rooms full of drunks just like these before, and at all too young an age. She lifted her chin, taking care to meet no one's eyes, and looked around the room. "Ah. I see someone I know. You two pick up what you can. Babak, Agape, the same but from the slaves. Stay alert. Shout for help if you need it." She glanced around the room again. "Even if you just think you might."

Dub and Is faded off to either side and Tetisheri ignored the lascivious glances cast her way as she crossed to a couch in the corner where Cornelia Metella sat, wine cup in hand, blessedly alone. "Lady."

Cornelia nodded. "Lady." She raised her cup as if to sip. From behind it she said, "What on earth are you doing here? I can't imagine even your mistress requiring your presence at one of these events."

A slave paused next to them and Tetisheri accepted a cup of wine, like Cornelia only pretending to sip at it. "One of what?"

Cornelia nodded at the impluvium. "At some point soon, our esteemed host Laurus will return, got up as the Lord of Misrule, and will ask all the ladies present to place their amulets in that bowl. After which he will invite all the men to pluck one out. The lady belonging to the amulet will spend the rest of the evening with the gentleman holding her amulet."

Tetisheri stared at her.

Cornelia nodded. "Oh, yes."

Tetisheri took a real gulp of wine this time. "Willingly?"

"Indeed, although—" Cornelia cast a disparaging eye around the room "—one can scarcely credit it, given the talent on offer."

Tetisheri pulled herself together. "One might ask what on earth you are doing here yourself, lady."

"One might." Cornelia's lips pressed together in a thin line. She pointed with her chin. "I was informed that this was a dinner party, and that Sextus would be here. He is. I had hoped to speak with him, but…"

Tetisheri followed her gaze to a skinny youth barely out of his teens who wasn't waiting for bowls and amulets to press his advances on the woman, ah, women, sharing his couch. One of them was old enough to be his mother and the other looked like enough to be her daughter.

Tetisheri realized she was staring. "It's like watching a chariot wreck in a race at the Hippodrome."

Cornelia sighed. "It is difficult to look away."

Somehow Tetisheri found the strength, and turned back to Cornelia, surprising a look of equal parts disgust and sadness on her face. It occurred to Tetisheri that whoever had informed Cornelia of Sextus' presence here this evening also must have known exactly what kind of Saturnalia festivity their host had in store for his guests. Tetisheri, remembering Cornelia's current lodging and who had made it available to her, thought she could make a pretty good guess as to that person's identity. "Juba," she said, without meaning to.

"He seems to believe that since I won't make myself available to him, I may as well make myself available to everyone else in Cyrene."

"Your guards…"

"I have none."

"But surely, the two men I saw outside your house…?"

Cornelia said nothing, and Tetisheri's suspicions were confirmed.

An explosion of sound and motion caused both women to start. A fat man in a toga kilted to fatter knees, with a lopsided laurel wreath drooping over one brow, pranced into the room, waving a tintinnabulum in the shape of Mercury. Mercury proudly sported an erect penis as long as one of his arms. It was festooned with red ribbons, presumably to match the bowl for the amulets and the slaves' tunics. "Children of Aristippus of Cyrene, the time has come to take your pleasure! Ladies, your amulets, please! Don't be shy! Yes, yes, come forward, place it there in the bowl! Yes, that's it, well done!" The bells on the tintinnabulum tinkled when Laurus used it to smack a tittering woman on the behind, and then paused to rub the figure of Mercury and his overlarge penis suggestively over the crack in her buttocks, to the loud encouragement of everyone watching.

He went all the way around the room—he skipped Sextus' couch, where matters had progressed with both ladies seeing service—and the finesse with which he put Mercury to work never improved. One woman opened her mouth willingly when Laurus raised Mercury to her lips. The level of noise increased as he went. Men called out encouragement and women gave fake screams of protest, some of them fighting to be first to cast their amulets into the bowl.

A few seemed less willing. One girl, who couldn't have been more than fourteen, shrank from the Lord of Misrule's attentions, until her much older companion encouraged her in Laurus' direction with a firm shove. She suffered the caress of the tintinnabulum and staggered into the pool. She wrenched off her amulet, flinging it into the bowl, after which she used the front of her tunic to mop up her tears.

This scene was entirely too familiar to Tetisheri, the survivor of a marriage to a man who could have given Laurus lessons in how to debauch the young and innocent.

"And he's her husband. The older gentleman." Cornelia stood up and set aside her wine cup. "This is where I take my leave. You should, too."

"Indeed." But over Cornelia's shoulder she saw Babak gesturing at her from the door leading to the inside of the house. "Excuse me, my page—"

"On your own head be it."

Cornelia stalked through the crowd like the Tenth Legion through Gaul, drawing every eye, and such was her righteous demeanor and imperious attitude that the roisterers fell back before her, almost (but not quite) ashamed. They might even have been awed.

Tetisheri would like to learn to walk like that one day. She shook herself and made her way to Babak's side.

"Urania?" Babak peered around her, very wide of eye. "You wished to speak to her?"

She shifted to block his view. "Yes. Where is she?"

"The cucina, lady. Follow me."

It was a relief to leave the noise and what was inspiring it behind. She followed Babak down the hallway, through an impressively sized and many-columned peristylium— arms dealing must be quite the lucrative profession—to the door of a smaller room, where slaves were washing dishes and cleaning pots under the supervision of a stout woman carrying a large wooden spoon as a badge of office, one she didn't hesitate to use to encourage efficiency in those under her authority. Tetisheri and Babak stopped just outside, looking in, their presence hidden in the shadows of the hallway.

One woman stood alone in back, scraping dough from the table top. She was dressed no better than the others, a stained tunic of indeterminate hue that had shrunk to above her ankles. The garment did nothing to hide her looks. Babak was right, she was beautiful. And she looked very familiar, especially that pale, finely textured skin and the thick braid of brown hair down her back.

"All right, that's enough!" the cook said. "They'll be busy for the rest of the night. They won't want anything but wine now. You filled the pitchers on your way out, yes? Good. Take yourself off to your beds, then, and mind you fold your tunics away safely for next year. And here." She opened a jar and began tossing iced buns into eager hands. "Urania's finest. I saved some for you."

The slaves went gossiping on their way. "Did you see that pig, Cassian? His new wife's your age, if not younger—"

"Do you see Sextus going at the widow Zosime and her daughter?"

"I saw. Better him than me. Gods."

A shout came from the atrium. "Urania! Urania! We want Urania!"

The group of slaves paused, looking over their shoulders. The cook made a shooing motion with her spoon and they shuffled off, conversation muted so as not to attract attention.

But Tetisheri did hear one girl whisper, "Poor Urania."

And another, "Better her than us."

"Laurus, bring her out! We haven't seen her for an age!"

"We haven't had her for longer than that!"

There was a gust of laughter. It sounded hard and lewd and to Tetisheri unmerciful. "Urania! Uraaaania! Come out, come out, wherever you are, come out and play with us!"

The cook looked at the woman cleaning the pastry table.

"You're wanted. You'd better clean yourself up and get out there."

The woman went on scraping dough.

"Look, my dear, you're a slave just like the rest of them and you do what you're told." She looked at Urania, not without sympathy. "It's only one night."

"Then you do it."

The cook fetched Urania a slap that nearly knocked her off her feet. "Get yourself cleaned up. The sooner you get out there, the sooner it's over with."

Urania straightened and started scraping the table again.

The cook sighed. "If you won't do it for yourself, then do it for—"

A patter of feet behind Tetisheri and one of the older slaves pushed past, disregarding Tetisheri and Babak. "Uraniaaaaa," he said, mocking the way the men in the atrium were calling her name. "You're wanted." He sniggered, his eyes running up and down her body.

Tetisheri wanted to tear them out of his head.

The cook shook her head. "Do as you wish. I'm off to my own bed." The slave, still sniggering, followed her.

Urania stood with her head bowed, her shoulders hunched, her hands clenched on the scraper.

Tetisheri walked forward into the light. Urania heard her and her head came up. There were no tears on her cheeks, Tetisheri saw. Like the women of Troy, she had wept for these things once already.

Whatever Tetisheri's thoughts had been as regards this woman, gaining her assent to flight, making a plan, hiding their tracks, finding a hiding place for her until she could be gotten safely out of Cyrene, ensuring that she and Neb and the Owls and Dub and Is and the *Hapi II* and its crew were not under arrest or attainder before they were safely away, all of it had flown right out the window when she heard the first man call Urania's name. She said in a low voice, "I'm a friend of your sister's."

Urania stared at her. "My sister?"

"Yes."

Urania's mouth opened and closed. "My sister?"

"Yes. She sent me here to find you and bring you to her."

Urania's stupefaction broke and she laughed, although there was no amusement in the sound. "Oh, I see. Someone sent you to me, to trick me into leaving all this—" she gestured at the kitchen and made an obscene gesture in the direction of the atrium "—so I can serve my pastries and my body to your master instead? Thanks, but no thanks. At least here the cook is decent."

"She hit you."

Urania sneered. "She could have hit me a lot harder, but she knew Laurus would have her beaten for damaging the goods."

They stared at each other. Into the silence Tetisheri said in a voice barely above a whisper, "Your nickname for her when you were children was Pipi."

Urania stood up straight, eyes startled. Her lips parted. She tried to speak and couldn't. She cleared her throat and tried again, her voice a painful rasp. "And her nickname for me?"

"Ranny."

Urania's eyes closed for a moment, and opened again. "If you are lying to me," she said fiercely, "I will kill you, do you understand me? I will tear out your entrails with my own hands. If they kill me for it I will kill you first!"

"Don't raise your voice," Tetisheri said, barely attending. "Is there a back way out of this house?"

"Yes." Tetisheri looked down to see Agape standing next to her. "There is a door in the wall in back of the kitchen garden."

"Isn't it locked?"

Agape's smile was a mere baring of teeth. "Not anymore."

Truly did the child have unexpected depths. Tetisheri looked back at Urania. "This is Agape, and this is Babak. My name is Tetisheri and they are in my service. Go with them."

"But I—I can't, I have to—"

"Or you can stay, and I'll tell Pipi you'd rather play party favor for Laurus than join her in Alexandria. It makes no difference to me."

That was a lie if she'd ever told one, but the brutality of her words shook Urania free of her paralysis. "I—I—yes, I'll go with you."

"Good. Follow these two. They will lead you to me. It's best that we're not seen leaving together."

Babak tugged at Tetisheri's palla. "Lady, you must come with us! You can't go out the way you came in! Those people—"

"I have to find Is and Dub." She gave him a tight smile. "Don't worry, they'll take care of me."

He did not look reassured. Agape glared at him. "They're going to come looking for her, Babak! We should go! Now!"

Tetisheri turned and ran back down the hallway. She dodged around one of the columns in the peristylium, a second, and before she gained the third felt two arms like iron lift her off her feet, one hand over her mouth. She was carried into the darkest corner of the room, behind some dense bush that flowered even in winter.

She didn't bother trying to scream, not in this house, but she fought, kicking, clawing, trying to bite his hand. She was slammed up against a wall for her pains. A voice in her ear said savagely, "Stop it, you little idiot! Ouch! Sobek's balls! Will you stop or am I going to have to get rough?" His voice changed. "As I remember you liked it well enough that one time."

She froze.

He heaved a sigh. "That's better." He raised his hand from her mouth slightly, ready at a moment to slap it down again.

Her voice was the barest whisper of sound. "Apollodorus?"

"Who else?"

Apollodorus.

11

Waves of emotion flooded over her, relief of course, immediate, all-consuming, rendering her momentarily limp. Joy, bringing with it a light-headedness that made her dizzy. And then? Sheer rage. She wanted to hit him again. She wanted to bite him. So she did, she bit his hand, hard.

"Ouch! Sheri, don't you know me?"

She wrenched her face free of his hand. "Yes, I know you," she hissed, keeping her voice as low as his. "Where in the seven hells have you been?"

It was so dark in the corner that she could barely make out his features. The scent of the flowers blooming in the shrub next to them perfumed the air with a delicate scent. All she could hear was his breath, all she could feel was the rise and fall of his breast against hers.

They stared at each other through the gloom, and then

both of them lunged forward at once. He wasn't in armor and his body was so hard and so hot against her own. He smelled so like Apollodorus, a musky scent both tart and sweet. She wanted to lick him all over. She wanted to climb him like a tree. She did climb him, one leg around him after the other, until she had her ankles firmly crossed in the small of his back. She yanked at his tunic. "Get it off!"

"Hold on a second, you little wildcat, let me—" Her hand found him and he groaned. "All right, if that's the way you want it but this is going to be over fast."

"I don't care! Hurry!" She felt cold air against her legs and the fluid coating her thighs and he kneed her open and pressed up against her, probing.

"By all the gods, girl, you have missed me." He pressed forward, his way made easy by her need.

"Ahhhhh." The sound she made was so nearly a shout that he covered her mouth again, this time with his own, devouring her with lips and teeth and tongue. She reveled in it. It was forever since she had felt like this. It was the day before.

"Yes, I have missed you, Apollodorus, oh how I have missed you." She felt her hips begin to move of their own accord, savoring the strength of his thrust, the heat and weight of him inside her, moving so surely, so steadily in search of their pleasure, whose end they both knew so well.

This was like nothing she had witnessed in the atrium. Here was no greed or lechery or degradation. Here was love and passion and need and trust. She wanted to laugh. She wanted to weep.

"Ah, gods, Sheri." He bit her neck where it joined her shoulder and that sharp pain was enough to send her over the edge and her back arched and her legs tightened, locking him to her, to her and no one else. Dimly she heard his growl of satisfaction,

They stood there, locked together, unmoving. His breath was rapid in her ear. She turned her lips to his throat, sucking at the beat of his blood in the vein there.

He half laughed, half groaned. "Nice to see you, too." He pulled his head back. She saw the flash of his teeth. "Keep that up, we'll be spending the rest of the night right here. And somehow I don't think that would be the best idea." His voice hardened. "Someone is bound to discover us and want their turn. What are you doing here, Tetisheri?"

She let her legs slip down over his hips to the floor. They were unsteady under her at first and she leaned against him, her ear against his chest. There was gilt or some such stuff on his tunic. Scratchy. She didn't care. Then his last question registered and she shoved him with both hands, which moved him back not at all. "Never mind me! What are you doing here, Apollodorus?"

He huffed out half a laugh. "That's my girl, always on the attack. Let me just—"

He pulled back and produced a kerchief. He took his time cleaning her up. He finished up with a soft suckling kiss that lingered and she had to bite her lip to keep from moaning. "Just marking my spot," he said, coming back to his feet, sounding so smug she wanted to hit him again. He cleaned up himself and arranged their tunics into some semblance of decency. Her palla had been lost in the mad rush to the corner and he found it and draped it around her shoulders, taking the opportunity to kiss her again.

"You are trying to change the subject," she said, her eyes closing in spite of herself.

"No indeed, lady. I missed you, too. Trust that if you trust nothing else."

She sighed. "You know I do. But what are you doing here?"

"Here, in Cyrene? I'm tasked by our queen to monitor Juba's inclinations in the coming war. In pursuit of such, I have, ah, wormed my way into his palace guard."

"Thank you. That I could have figured out for myself. What are you doing in this house this evening?"

He sighed. They were still half standing, half leaning against the wall, bodies pressed together, he as unwilling to part as she. "I am here in this house this evening because my watch commander tasked me with having the back of that feckless puppy, Sextus, to make sure he doesn't bloody his own nose. It's a duty none of us relishes, so our commander does us the favor of rotating that duty among us. My number came up." He muttered something uncomplimentary that she decided not to hear. "Now. What are you doing here?"

"I, amazingly, am not sent here by our queen."

He said nothing. He said it eloquently.

"It's true," she said even as she wondered if it was. "I have her permission to absent myself from duty in order to accompany Uncle Neb."

"And Neb is here because—"

"There is no silphium to be found in the Emporeum in Alexandria, and we have had no word from our factor here."

He was silent for a moment. "I see. And you're here, in this house, because—"

"We had news of a gathering of Cyrene's elite—" he snorted "—and came to ferret out any news we could."

He snorted again. "And you say you are not here on business of the queen."

"I'm not! Well. Not officially."

"Oh, I completely understand."

She would have pinched him but then she remembered. "Urania!"

"Who?"

She wrestled free of his grasp. "I have to—I'm meeting—Agape and Babak need me, I must go." She frowned. "No, wait, I must find Is and Dub."

"No fear," came a drawl from behind a distant column. She didn't have to see him to be aware he was smirking. "We're never that far away."

Tetisheri had been embarrassed so many times by all Five Soldiers separately and together that she was inured to it by now. Mostly. She did find herself stamping her foot. "Am I never to have any privacy with you lot around?" It sounded rote even to her own ears.

The smirk was entirely gone as Dub strolled forward. "Not in this house, Sheri."

Apollodorus caught her hand. "Wait. Where's Neb?"

"He didn't come back in time to join us."

"Back from where?"

"He left early this afternoon to find Timur's house. He will have returned by now, and all the better for having missed this bacchanal." She stood on tiptoe to kiss him. "We're at the Waterfront."

He caught her face in his hands. "I know."

She put her lips to his ear. "I have a very comfortable bed behind a door with a lock on it."

Again the flash of white teeth. "How thick are the walls?"

Dub led them to Is, who was standing guard over a side door that led outside without going through the atrium. The screams and shouts from that room had diminished but were still loud enough to hide any sound of their passage. It appeared they had forgotten about Urania, at least temporarily. Best to be gone before they remembered.

Apollodorus risked a peep around the door and returned, shaking his head. "The only thing young Sextus is at risk of is catching the pox. Let's get out of here."

They emerged into a garden where every bush was sculpted into a shape never seen in nature. The benches spread between them were overly ornate and looked incapacitatingly uncomfortable. Is made a sound of disgust. "No wonder he holds his orgy inside. You could break bones humping on one of these."

The front doors still stood wide open to all comers, so to speak. They found their cabrio driver dicing with the others outside the gate. He swept up a handful of change—at least someone had gotten lucky that evening—and trotted off to where his horse drowsed with a feed bag over his nose.

Tetisheri let the men go ahead, pausing beneath the

shadow of a tree. "Babak?" she said, keeping her voice to a whisper. "Agape?"

They coalesced out of the darkness, Urania with them. She carried a large bundle wrapped in a ragged blanket, the corners knotted behind her back. Tetisheri shepherded the three of them toward the cabrio. Urania halted when she saw all the men. "Who are they?"

"Friends. They mean you no harm."

"But—"

Tetisheri pushed her forward. "Could we please get out of here before your master realizes you aren't forming part of the evening's entertainment after all?"

The look Urania shot Tetisheri, even in the gloom of night, told her that she and Urania weren't destined to become friends.

The two Owls tumbled into carriage. Dub offered Urania a hand. She pulled back and he dropped his, indicating the seat. "Sit here, lady."

Tetisheri wondered if Urania had ever been addressed with courtesy in her adult life.

"Up you go, Sheri," Apollodorus said from behind her, and lifted her up and in. He settled in next to her, arm holding her close to his side. "All ready? Is, be more room if you sat on the floor."

Is sighed. "Always the floor, never the seat. Story of my life."

The cabrio snapped the reins and they lurched off.

None of the three men evinced the slightest curiosity as regards to Urania. But then they'd known Tetisheri for a long time.

Just when she thought she could perhaps stop listening for a hue and cry from the mob following them, the cabrio took them too quickly around a corner. The carriage raised up on two wheels and thumped down again, jostling the passengers. A plaintive murmur came from the bundle at Urania's breast.

"What...?" Tetisheri stared at the bundle, and accusingly at Urania. Urania stared back defiantly and gathered the bundle closer to her, obviously prepared to defend its contents with her life.

Tetisheri looked from Urania to Babak and Agape, on the floor on either side of Is. Babak wouldn't meet her eyes but Agape did, chin raised, daring Tetisheri to make any comment. "She wouldn't leave without her and I don't blame her."

Is started to chuckle, and gathered an Owl beneath each arm. "So now we know why you ordered a larger carriage, Tetisheri."

"Not that large!" She looked back at Urania, realization dawning. "And that's why you wouldn't come when Ca— when Pipi sent for you the first time."

"The man she sent said there was no room for a child. Myself, such was his character that if I went with him I didn't think we would ever see Alexandria, anyway." She pulled the covering from the child's hair, and Nut shone her silvery benevolence down on both of them, mother and daughter, as like as sisters. She kissed the child's forehead and looked back up at Tetisheri.

If you won't do it for yourself, the cook had said, *then do it for—*

This was who she had meant. Tetisheri remembered that

young girl in tears as she placed her amulet in the bowl and felt a wave of nausea. For Laurus, it would only have been a matter of time before he offered up Urania's daughter to his guests.

Tetisheri held Urania's eyes and gave a single, slow, grave nod. It was as good as swearing an oath.

Urania took it as one.

At Tetisheri's direction they drew up a little way down the street from the inn and they entered separately, first Is and Dub, then Babak and Agape with Urania and her daughter swathed in Tetisheri's blue palla, looking like a woman of substance instead of a mother and child. Apollodorus and Tetisheri came last, he dignified and maybe a little threatening in Juba's gilt-encrusted livery walking behind her, she imitating Cornelia Metella's privileged arrogance as best she could. The common room was shut off with a low murmur of late drinkers leaking out from beneath the door. The only person Tetisheri saw was a half-awake scullion pretending to sweep the floor. Staying in character she took no notice of him, and didn't relax until they were up the stairs and the door of the suite had closed behind them.

Neb was sitting at the table in front of the window, nursing a cup of something, and such was her instant relief upon seeing him that she almost broke into a run. "Uncle! Where were you? We waited until we couldn't—"

She skidded to a halt as a man standing outside the window stepped back into the room. He smiled at her. "Lady Tetisheri, what a pleasant surprise."

Neb's voice was wooden. "I believe you know Aurelius Cotta."

The pearl suspended from the tip of his beard was standing at attention.

Well, what would Cornelia Metella do? Tetisheri stiffened her spine. "That will be all, thank you," she said to the air.

There was a chorus of obedient murmurs followed by a bustle of movement and the sounds of doors opening and closing. Apollodorus, she knew without looking, had vanished out the door to the hallway before she had spoken and was even now moving rapidly in the direction of whichever barracks Juba saw fit to house his personal guard in.

Yet another reason to add to the long list of reasons for her intense dislike of Aurelius Cotta. She straightened her shoulders and went to stand behind Uncle Neb's chair, ignoring the seat Cotta had pulled out for her. There was something about Aurelius Cotta that could never allow her to relax in his presence. Her uncle's shoulder, too, was tense beneath her hand.

"Allow me," Cotta said, and poured her a cup of wine without asking.

His habit of playing the host beneath roofs not his own had always grated, but she accepted the cup with a stiff nod and barely wet her lips before setting the cup down.

He noticed, because Cotta always noticed everything. "I know, dreadful stuff, isn't it? Certainly nothing to compare with your cellar in Alexandria." He smiled. He smiled a lot, did Aurelius Cotta, and the expression was never reassuring.

There was a faint family resemblance to his more famous cousin, their difference forever distinguished by the scar that split his eyebrow and came perilously close to the corner of his eye, a scar gained when, as one unreliable legend had it, he took a blow meant for Caesar struck by Vercingetorix himself. He was Caesar's most trusted associate, left behind in Alexandria with a watching brief on Cleopatra and no doubt to gather any intelligence that might be useful to the self-styled Colossus of Rome. And most certainly to be available to collect any silver and gold Caesar might ask Cleopatra to liberate from her royal treasury and donate to Caesar's current cause.

Cotta was a soldier; very well, she would go on the attack. "It's late and I'm very tired." That was easy because it was the truth. It was also true that she didn't have to fake a yawn. "We are flattered and honored by your presence, Aurelius Cotta, as always. Is there something we may do for you before we retire for the night?"

"Alas," he said, radiating regret, "yes, I'm afraid there is. Your uncle and I were about to come to the point when you returned with your retinue." He leaned forward and lowered his voice, as if he were to impart information of great importance only they were entitled to hear. "Caesar is coming."

Tetisheri met his eyes with something she hoped looked like polite indifference. "He is expected."

Cotta allowed himself to be surprised into a laugh. "Indeed, it's hard to miss the ships of war in the harbor and the many recruits marching up and down the streets."

"We hear Scipio has as many as ten legions at his back."

"Rumor and exaggeration flourish before a battle."

"And that Caesar has fewer than three."

He gave a faint smile. "I'm afraid the more pressing problem is feeding the ones we have."

Tetisheri noticed in passing that he had returned an oblique answer to a remark meant only to needle, and conceded, reluctantly and not for the first time, that Cotta was a master at verbal fencing, far better than she would ever be. "Feeding them?" Next to her Nebenteru stirred, but he remained silent.

"A matter of supplies, lady. Juba has stripped the countryside to support his own and Scipio's armies. There is nothing left to forage from here to Carthage."

She was not quite the naif she was pretending to be. She knew as everyone knew that Roman armies marched on Egyptian grain.

When she said nothing he gestured at the door that led onto the balcony. "I was admiring your new ship. Nebenteru tells me she puts on an excellent turn of speed for a vessel of her size. You could be to Alexandria and back again before Caesar steps ashore."

The latest word, gathered in by Is and Dub in their perambulations about town, was that Caesar was in Sicily. Weather permitting, he could be mere days, even hours, away from landing in Africa. In fact the battle could be won or lost and well over before completing the round trip between Cyrene and Alexandria. "The *Hapi II* is only one ship, and Caesar has many thousands of soldiers to feed."

"The *Hapi II* is not the only ship I am commandeering, nor is Alexandria the only port to which I am sending them."

I am commandeering. Gloves off, then. "We have no choice in the matter? We are merchants of Alexandria, Aurelius Cotta. We are not soldiers in the Roman army."

"Ah. You think your queen would refuse Caesar this boon, then?"

All three of them knew perfectly well that Cleopatra would do no such thing. Goaded, Tetisheri said, "Juba knows you are here, I expect?"

It was a crude threat but a real one. Juba would be delighted to have a hostage to play with. Even better, to tell Caesar he had.

Cotta smiled again. "And what would your queen say to that, lady?"

She looked at her uncle. He was concentrating on the small oil lamp he held in his hands, turning it around and around and around, without ceasing. His skin was shiny with residue from the oil.

Cotta knocked one fist against the table top. "It's settled then. A quick trip to Alexandria. Your uncle will leave tomorrow morning."

"No." Nebenteru spoke for the first time.

Cotta looked at him. "I beg your pardon?"

Uncle Neb put the lamp to one side. He placed his hands flat on the table and met Cotta's eyes with a cold stare of his own.

Tetisheri was amazed. She hadn't known Uncle Neb could look like that.

Neb spoke without looking away from Cotta. "We have business in Cyrene that will keep us here through the next two days. The earliest we could depart will be the third morning hence."

His party, Tetisheri thought.

Cotta's hesitation was barely noticeable. Then he relaxed and she knew he'd made the decision to give in gracefully. That, or he knew the exact date of Caesar's landing and there was more time in hand than he was letting on. "As you wish." He brushed an invisible crumb from the table top. "Of course, the lady Tetisheri will remain here in Cyrene while you, Neb, make the trip to Alexandria."

Did Cotta really imagine for one moment that Neb would not return for her? She hoped her contempt for his judgement didn't show.

On the other hand, she didn't care if it did.

"No," Neb said again, still in that tone that would not be crossed. "I will remain here. Tetisheri will take the *Hapi II* to Alexandria, load it with as much grain and foodstuffs as it can hold, and bring it back here to Cyrene."

"Not Cyrene." Cotta spoke automatically, his mind still processing this change.

Tetisheri watched Nebenteru. He had still not met her eyes. She would not contradict her uncle in front of Cotta, but there would be a conversation when Cotta left. If he ever did.

"Where then?"

"When you need to know, I will tell you. In fact, thinking it over, it would be best to delay your departure for a day or two."

"Two."

Neb was inflexible. She'd had no idea.

Cotta rapped the table top again. "We're reasonable people. No doubt we'll reach an accommodation that suits us all." He bowed briefly. "I'll be in touch."

Neb and Tetisheri remained where they were, watching him walk to the door. It closed gently behind him. His footsteps were soundless on the stairs.

Tetisheri turned to Neb. "You want me to take the *Hapi II* to Alexandria while you remain here?"

He set his jaw. The pearl at the tip of his beard quivered. "I will not leave you here alone."

"Is and Dub will be with me."

"Is and Dub will be with you when you return to Alexandria. I'll keep the Owls." He seemed to wake up. "Did I see Apollodorus here tonight?"

"You did, but don't call him that."

He blinked. "What should I call him?"

She thought back over the evening. "I don't know. We didn't get around to that. He's here on business of the queen."

Neb snorted. "He's been here since he left Alexandria?"

"I suppose so. We didn't talk about that, either."

"Well, what did you talk about?"

She felt her color rise. "We didn't have a chance to talk much."

"Was he at Laurus' party?"

"Yes. He's working in Juba's palace guard." They had their heads together, speaking in whispers.

The pearl positively vibrated. "Juba was there?"

Tetisheri shook her head. "A guest of his. Apollodorus was his escort. Uncle Neb?"

"What?"

"What's the real reason you want me to leave?" He said nothing. "Wait. Is it that you want to stay?"

After a long moment, he sighed. "It is that I must, Tetisheri."

"Why? What do you mean? What happened today?" She thought. "Oh. Did you find Timur?"

"Yes."

"Oh, I'm so glad." She saw his expression. "Oh."

"He's dead, Tetisheri," Neb said heavily. "And that's not all."

There was a long silence following the end of his tale. He described the body he had found with Timur's and she said immediately, "Fulvio. Cotta's servant."

Neb's brow cleared. "Hah. I knew I knew him."

"He's Cotta's shadow and right-hand man."

The furrow on his brow returned. "Timur was tortured. Fulvio was only killed." He closed his eyes briefly. "Only. Gods." He opened his eyes again. "It was professionally done, Sheri."

"Which?"

"Both."

"I don't understand." Tetisheri was frowning at her tightly clasped hands. "What was Fulvio doing at Timur's house?"

She raised her head and they stared at each other.

When she spoke again it was to what she perceived to be the most immediate of their concerns. "Does Cotta know?"

He shook his head. "He made no mention of it, and I'm sure he would have."

"Perhaps. Perhaps not. He is the past master of an implied threat. If he knows, it's a sword over your head he can swing when it would best suit his plans." She thought for a moment. "You should take the *Hapi II* back to Alexandria."

"No."

"But—"

"My dear," he said with a finality that silenced her. "No. I will not leave you here. War is coming. It's possible Caesar could even besiege this city."

"Surely the battle will take place nearer to Carthage?"

He was implacable. "We don't know that, and not knowing only makes the situation worse."

"Apollodorus is here."

"He won't be when the fighting begins. Everything I've seen, everything I've heard, since we stepped on shore leads me to believe that Juba has allied himself with Scipio."

She had no answer. Everything she had heard and seen had led her to believe the same thing, including Sextus Pompey's presence at Laurus' orgy. Juba would want to keep his Roman guests happy.

One thing was certain: there was no arguing with her uncle in this obdurate mood. "I should tell you about the party at Laurus' house." She took a deep breath, and began.

He listened without comment until she came to the end but she could see that it was an effort. He looked down and saw that his fists had clenched. He unclenched them, one finger at a time.

"No," he said, enunciating each word with care. "You will not remain behind as Cotta's hostage for my good behavior. His thought is all for Caesar. He will waste no care on you or anyone else." He closed his eyes briefly and shook his head. "After all, I've seen it all before, haven't I."

He looked at her. "It isn't just the war itself that ruins us, Sheri. The anticipation, the fear, the dread before ever the first sword drawn, it affects everyone. The kind of thing you witnessed this evening was common in Alexandria during our war, ending in rape and theft and murder and riot in the streets. In the cities along the river, too, at least those on the delta, who saw more than their share of Roman legionnaires marching back and forth and reacted just as rashly as you might expect with the cohorts eating up all their supplies and seducing all their women. At least Caesar brought order back to the city, and to the river." He looked out the window. "You can smell the same here. The thrill, and the terror. It will lead to the worst excesses."

"Will you cancel your reception?"

He shook his head. "No, I will not. It would be noticed. We don't need to draw any more attention than we already have."

She spoke her thought out loud. "And we can't just up and leave." She looked at him. "Can we."

He huffed out a breath. "Would you like to carry that news to our queen? How would she react, do you think? Even you, Tetisheri, her oldest, her most trusted friend, might be subject to her displeasure. Which I imagine would be severe She sees herself as Caesar's wife. Caesarion is Caesar's son. He may one day be Caesar's heir. She would expect us to do everything in our power to support him. You know this to be true."

His reasoning was not unsound, although an impending war seemed to be adequate reason for anyone to decamp the area. She thought of Fulvio, and of Timur, and of Cotta and of the information Is and Dub had shared with them over breakfast. "Have you sent an invitation to the lady Cornelia Metella, Uncle?"

"Who? Oh. Scipio's sister. She's here?"

"Yes. Will you send her an invitation to your party? I'll take it to her."

He eyed her suspiciously. "Why?"

She told him.

He heaved a gust of a sigh. To the table he said, "On the third morning from now, you will be aboard the *Hapi II* on your way back to Alexandria. Am I understood?"

"You are." She stood up and stooped to put her arms around his neck. After a moment he returned her embrace. "I love you, Uncle." She kissed his forehead.

"And I love you, my dear. You are the light of my life."

She drew back, smiling. "The *Hapi II* is the light of your life."

And her heart lifted when he laughed.

12

The next morning a caterer appeared with a cook, a baker, and kitchen staff in tow and began to receive orders of food, wine, and beer. Suppliers carried in crates loaded with glassware and dinnerware, linens, padded stools and chairs, candles and candelabra, and all the rest of the items that Neb, a consummate host, considered at minimum absolutely essential for the success of the event.

No couches, Tetisheri noticed. Good. She was rather off couches for social events.

Another purveyor appeared with a cart full of plinths of various heights, and Neb fussed around placing them just so, close enough together to give the impression of plenty and far enough apart to provide space for admiring groups to gather around each of them. Which was followed by a stream of the *Hapi II*'s oarsmen, pressed into service as longshoremen, ferrying items of cargo between inn and moorage. He'd brought the good stuff, too, Tetisheri thought: illustrated editions of *The Iliad* and *The Odyssey*, always appealing to those who liked to have such things on display for visitors to see and admire; a selection of the rarer herbs (no silphium, of course) in beautifully carved cedar boxes (presentation was all); a small lyre carved from ivory suitable for a child just beginning her musical education; a magnificent collar of gold and lapis with matching earrings that would convince any wearer she was or at least looked like the direct descendent of Nefertari. There were exotic vases made of burnished copper from Britannia in the north and rare jewels and bolts of silk from Punt in the east.

There was also an official of the city, one Plinius, who greeted Neb with a welcoming smile and then informed him that to host an event at which goods would be sold—

"Might be sold," Neb said.

Another big smile, this one frankly disbelieving—to host such an event required an agent registered with the authorities of Cyrene, and would Neb step this way for a moment?

At that moment a trio of musicians arrived and erected a small dais in one corner. They mounted it, tuned up lutes and flutes and tambours and began rehearsing, popular airs that everyone could hum along to as well as classical tunes familiar to everyone else. Their manager dodged around the room, shouting at them from various corners, "That last verse isn't quite clear!" and "That tambour sounds as if it's being banged against the wall!"

"No dancing girls?" Tetisheri said, knowing very well what his answer would be.

Neb, still ruffled after his chat with Plinius, spoke with a snap. "Certainly not. We don't need anyone flinging their feet and hands around the displays."

Tetisheri hid a smile. Neb considered anything that detracted from admiration of their stock to be unnecessary to the ambiance. "How much do we owe the tax man?"

He glowered and told her. She gulped. "Well. Not quite as large a profit as we had imagined, then."

Something nagged at the back of her mind, something about Timur, but before she could hunt it down and pin it to the wall of her consciousness their landlord bustled up, flushed and flustered, overcome by the magnitude of the event being hosted beneath his roof. He made sure everyone knew its name, and his, too. Tactfully, Neb drew him into the melee, giving him tasks enough to make him feel needed. Neb told Tetisheri later than the landlord had dropped only one crate of glassware, which they both considered a cheap price to pay.

Urania and the child kept to their room, Urania looking terrified every time she heard the door opening. Tetisheri made sure they had food and water, and sent Babak and Agape separately to the market, wearing neither their Owl nor House Nebenteru insignia, to shop for new clothes for them, after which she tasked Babak with disappearing their old rags out of the inn, somewhere to be burned to ashes. "And stir the ashes afterward."

"Yes, lady." This was the first time any of the Owls had been involved in Tetisheri's side venture. They asked no questions and appeared pretty sanguine overall, and yet again she sent up a prayer thanking Bast for the gift of intelligent servants.

Is and Dub disappeared early to continue their exploration of the city to take the pulse of residents and visitors alike. The visitors were mostly armed, the residents mostly alarmed, so—Neb said sourly—business as usual in any city on the eve of war. Rumor was rife, and the two Soldiers judged that most of it was about as reliable as rumor usually was. Caesar had landed five miles to the north of the city with twenty legions and an overwhelming amount of cavalry. In a surprise move Juba had thrown in his lot with Caesar, but no, he and Scipio had marched north in an attack that surprised and confounded Caesar as he landed, driving him back into the sea, drowning him and his troops. The battle had already been fought, Caesar had won. The battle had already been fought, Scipio and Juba had won. The battle had already been fought to a stalemate, with tremendous losses on both sides and no resolution in sight (by far the most likely of the rumors, they all agreed). The dead were rotting where they had fallen and starvation and disease both would be rampant across the countryside and soon the city itself.

"You couldn't rent a cart for a thousand denarii today," Dub said, "and all the stables have hired armed guards."

Neb looked worried. "Are people leaving?"

Is shook his head. "Just making sure they can if they have to."

On the whole, Tetisheri was relieved. The louder the rumor of war was, the less notice would be taken of minor incidents like escaping slaves and anyone who might be helping them.

There was no word from Apollodorus. She imagined the

conditions prevailing in Juba's court at present would be fraught, if not downright manic, and refused to worry.

Well, she tried. After that she hired a cabrio for three times the amount she had paid before and called on Cornelia.

"Ah. I see you escaped Laurus safely."

"As did you."

The patrician nose elevated a fraction. "I retired in good order and with no loss of dignity."

Tetisheri remembered the young wife being forced into public adultery by her husband and had no desire to laugh. "Forgive me, lady. You did indeed. We are both to be congratulated." She reached into the purse fastened at her waist and extended a scroll, addressed to Cornelia in Neb's broad hand. "I bring you an invitation."

"Do you?" Cornelia read it and raised an eyebrow. "Another Saturnalia revel?"

"I would think one of those per season should be quite enough."

"More than enough." Cornelia poured tea.

"Thank you." Tetisheri sipped, and shared some of the rumors brought back by Is and Dub.

The patrician nose elevated itself again. "Rabble."

"I can't argue with that. But my uncle insists I leave with the *Hapi II* the day after tomorrow."

"He is wise. Better always to be in advance of the mob if at all possible. One never knows what they will do. And Gaius is known for turning his legionnaires loose on a conquered population for a few days, before he comes striding in to restore order and play the rescuing hero."

Tetisheri looked through the window at the garden, its figures formed of obscenities she had been forced to witness in person two nights before. "The *Hapi II* is a new ship," she said idly.

"Oh?"

"And very comfortable." Her eyes met Cornelia's, and she added without emphasis, "And commodious."

Cornelia busied herself with refilling her cup. It was porcelain, glazed a rosy white, the lip formed in the likeness of a woman's nude torso, arms outspread. Tetisheri's was its mate. In a style complementary to the house, and a reminder, if either of them needed it, what was meant by Cornelia's residence there. "Where will you be sailing to?"

"Alexandria."

"Ah. Not Rome, then."

Tetisheri shrugged. "All ports in the Middle Sea are available from Alexandria."

A faint smile. "True enough."

It was impossible to read from Cornelia's demeanor if she was truly Juba's guest here in Cyrene, free to come and go as she chose, or his prisoner. Everything Tetisheri knew about Juba told her he was determined to despoil instantly anything Roman that came within reach. No better object lesson could have been served than the luring of a Roman woman of Cornelia's stature to Laurus' festivities. See how much worse it could be? he was telling her. A Roman woman of the patrician class and spotless reputation, the granddaughter of two consuls and one praetor, Pompey's widow and Scipio's sister, that was enticing enough. She was also an attractive woman, and so far as Tetisheri knew one of the few Caesar had yet to seduce. That fact alone would make her irresistible to Juba.

Tetisheri was fairly certain getting Cornelia Metella safely away from Juba's attentions was why the Eye of Isis was currently present in Cyrene. She could be wrong, let's not forget that. But she didn't think so.

"The day after tomorrow, did you say?"

"Yes. Uncle Neb wanted both of us to host the party, so we set sail a little before dawn the next morning." Tetisheri set down her cup and kept her voice deliberately noncommittal. "In a stroke of sheer genius, my uncle has secured a moorage directly across dockside from our inn." She smiled. "He's very proud of her. I expect he'll be giving the grand tour during our reception to anyone who wants a closer look."

"I expect everyone will want a closer look."

They sipped their tea. All very civilized on the surface, a veritable jungle full of claws and fangs beneath. "I wonder, lady, if I might be permitted the impertinence...?"

One perfectly groomed eyebrow went up. "Yes?"

"When last I was here, I passed a man coming in as I was leaving. I know him. One Fulvio. A Roman. In Caesar's service."

The second eyebrow went up to join the first. "In Aurelius Cotta's service, I believe you mean."

"Well, yes."

"Don't try so hard to look flustered, lady." Cornelia's voice was very dry. "It doesn't suit you."

Tetisheri swallowed a laugh. "I beg your pardon, lady. Very well. I wondered what his errand could be."

"And given who he works for, what on earth he is doing in the enemy camp?"

"Well, yes," Tetisheri said again. She felt that the other woman was a step and a half ahead of her and had been since Tetisheri had walked in the door.

Cornelia set down her cup. "He came to inquire if I had any news I would care to share of my brother's intentions."

"Ah." Tetisheri drank tea.

"I had to inform him that, alas, I haven't seen Quintus since Juba moved me here, and that at any rate he has never been one to share his thoughts with a woman." She reflected. "It was even the truth. If you had waited outside you would have seen Fulvio leave shortly after he arrived."

"I see." Tetisheri put her cup down. "Thank you."

Cornelia inclined her head briefly. "Was there anything else?"

"No, lady." Tetisheri got to her feet. "And I must be about my uncle's business. Thank you so much for receiving me this afternoon. I hope we will see you tomorrow."

"Perhaps." A faint smile. "It certainly sounds intriguing. One has heard of House Nebenteru's entertainments even in Rome."

Tetisheri gave a slight bow. "We are flattered."

Her cabrio was waiting, Babak inside with an anxious look on his face that eased when he saw her leave the house. He looked over her shoulder as she climbed in and said beneath his breath, "They're still there, lady. The guards we saw last time."

"I am aware." They hadn't stopped Cornelia from

attending Laurus' Saturnalia celebration, although that was probably on Juba's instructions. Would they stop Cornelia coming to Uncle Neb's reception tomorrow night when it wasn't?

Raising her voice she gave the driver directions for their next destination. Babak frowned. "Surely we must return to the inn, lady?"

"Surely we must," she said. "Almost immediately."

The neighborhood was as Nebenteru had reported, large homes on large lots, wonderful views of city and bay, quiet even during the day. A tradesman's cart sat in front of one house. Children could be heard shouting and laughing behind another. A cat meowed. The scent of baking bread wafted up the street. Her mouth watered. It had been a long time since breakfast.

Tetisheri recognized Timur's house from Neb's description, with the proud golden lion over the door. There was no movement that she could see other than shrubbery gently rustled by a faint, warm breeze. "Driver? Go down to the end of the street, please, and then drive back slowly." She leaned down and whispered in Babak's ear. "If you see something, don't show it, and say nothing. Wait until we are home."

He did as she asked. The clop of the horse's hooves were slow and deliberate and the wood of the carriage creaked a little. Just before passing Timur's house on their way back up the street she heard what sounded like the toe of a boot striking masonry, followed by a smothered curse. She looked up, elaborately casual, and let her eyes drift across the scene in front of her as the cabrio's horse plodded on up the road to the intersection. "A lovely neighborhood," she said, loud enough to be heard.

"Beautiful view," Babak said, playing along.

"I should mention the area to my uncle. We don't have a home in Cyrene. It might be worth looking into something here."

"Yes, lady," Babak said, running out of ideas.

They were nearly to the harbor when Tetisheri spoke again, this time in a low tone just above a whisper. "What did you see, Babak?"

"A man, lady. Hiding behind the house."

"What kind of man?"

"If I had to guess, a soldier. He wasn't in uniform but he wore a gladius."

"Did you see his face? Would you recognize him again?"

His eyes kindled. "Yes, lady. I would know him again."

"Yes," she said back, looking thoughtful. "So would I."

When they reached the harbor she roused herself. "Everyone is going to be tired tonight, Babak. Shall we bring them dinner?"

"We have food here, Urania. Come and eat."

"Can you bring us some?" A protesting murmur. "I'm

sorry, dearest. We must stay hidden. We don't want anyone to find us."

"We don't leave the apartment again this evening, Urania, and no one unknown or untrusted by us will be allowed in."

A stubborn silence. Tetisheri sighed. "All right. I'll have Agape and Babak bring you food and wine and water."

And empty the commode, she thought but didn't say.

13

The day dawned bright and clear, enough of a breeze blowing onshore to moderate the higher inland temperatures. Neb muttered a thank-you to Horus, and Zeus and Jupiter, too, in case Horus hadn't recognized he was being addressed the first time, and plunged into activity. He arranged and rearranged the rented tables, chairs, plinths, and candelabra, pressing everyone within arm's reach into service as muscle. Is and Dub soon made themselves scarce under the pretext of scavenging the city for news, so the brunt fell on Tetisheri, Babak, Agape, and their beleaguered landlord. Urania and the child remained locked behind the door of their room.

"I wish I was an escaped slave," Babak said in a low mutter.

Which was nevertheless loud enough to earn him a hiss from the other side of the room, where Agape struggled

167

to lift a plinth carved in the shape of a lotus blossom that wouldn't have looked out of place holding up the roof of an Egyptian temple circa Rameses II. "Don't even joke about a thing like that, Babak!"

Cowed, he kept the rest of his embittered thoughts to himself.

It was early afternoon before the receiving room was brought up to Neb's exacting standards. At their first opportunity the three of them deserted the inn for the streets and some fresh air, before Neb hailed them back inside to find fault with their dress clothes.

Babak, brightening, said, "If he doesn't like them, we don't have to go, right?"

Agape poked him. "The Lady of the Two Lands knows us by name. You don't get to whine."

Babak mumbled something that might have been "Why not?"

Tetisheri found a food cart that sold first-rate dolmas, two carts away from another that sold divine cakes made with spiced honey and chopped dates. They found a fountain with an unoccupied bench in front of it and sat, munching and watching the world go by.

The streets were even more congested than the day before. No one seemed to be buying or selling, although everyone seemed to be drinking. They were also, to a man, woman, and child, preoccupied with approaching everyone who appeared even remotely familiar to them and asking for news. Even fish, the dew hardly dry on their gladii, were not proof against entreaty—"Have you received orders?" "Where are you off to?" "Has Caesar come?" "How many legions did he bring?" "Is the Tenth with him?"

Babak licked his fingers free of the last bit of honey. "Why does everyone ask about the Tenth?"

"It's Caesar's favorite, allegedly."

But his attention had shifted. "Lady. Look."

A house cabrio with a uniformed driver pushed through the crowd with all the finesse of a wildebeest. Laurus, red-faced and furious, sat in the back. "Make way there! Make way!" His driver's shouts were mostly ineffectual, as people simply ignored them, avid in the pursuit of some news, any news of the day.

Tetisheri rose to her feet. "Let's see where Laurus is going."

Babak, who had bent his head the better to hear her low-voiced words above the cacophony of the crowd, vanished into the throng, Agape close behind him. Tetisheri followed at her leisure, certain in the knowledge that both Owls were keeping her in sight.

The chariot drew up before a nondescript building set back from the street. Laurus descended to the stone pavements and marched up the stairs, his belly bouncing beneath his tunic, and tripping only once over his hastily draped toga. All resemblance to the Lord of Misrule had vanished, replaced (deliberately, certainly) by a busy and important man very much aware of his status. The guard on the door leapt to attention and flung it open with a deep bow without even asking his identity.

Tetisheri maneuvered through the crowd to station herself within hearing distance of the portico. She was rewarded some fifteen minutes later when the door opened and Laurus emerged, followed by another man in a plain tunic with some sort of badge of office on his shoulder.

He was speaking rapidly, attempting—unsuccessfully it appeared—to placate this irate and imminent citizen. His words came clearly to Tetisheri's ears.

"I do beg your pardon again, sir. I quite take your concerns to be important, but at this present moment—" he looked out over the wave of humanity currently flooding the streets of the city "—it's all my men can do to keep order, not to mention discourage all our resident burglars from taking advantage of all those enticingly empty homes. I assure you that as soon as the present, er, situation resolves itself, I will send a patrol to your house to take your statement and interview your slaves."

Laurus looked the last thing from satisfied. "See that you do! I am in the confidences of men of the highest degree and I doubt any of them will take kindly to this indifference to the escape of a most valuable slave! Not to mention her child, who is also my property!"

"Quite right, sir," the officer said soothingly. He shepherded the infuriated arms dealer to the curb and nearly lifted him into his own cabrio. There was more muscle beneath that tunic than was apparent at first sight.

Laurus, entitled and indignant, did not thank him. "Drive on!"

"Make way, there! Make way!" his driver shouted, and the cabrio began edging into the maelstrom of other cabrios, carriages, and carts shoving and bumbling along on their own urgent missions.

The man in the tunic exchanged a speaking glance with the guard and vanished back inside.

"So Laurus has lost a slave, has he?" said a voice next to Tetisheri, who turned to see a woman standing next to her, an empty shopping basket on her arm, hair wrapped in a colorful swatch of fabric in the Nubian style. "Not a surprise, given the goings-on in that house." She gave a theatrical shudder.

"Goings-on?" Tetisheri said, eyes wide.

She was treated to a litany of activities for which Laurus was infamous, none of which surprised her but to which she responded with shocked gasps and murmurs of "No! I never heard of such a thing! Did you ever!"

Pleased with such a receptive audience and aware that other people standing nearby had begun listening, too, the housewife expanded on the theme until she had to pause to draw breath. In summation, she said, "While I'm a good, law-abiding citizen, it's no surprise to me that one of his slaves ran off."

Tetisheri allowed a puzzled frown to furrow her brow. "Odd."

The housewife looked at her. "What is odd?"

"Well." Tetisheri looked around the circle of inquiring faces, all primed for some new scandal to attach to Laurus' already infamous name. "This slave he is pursuing must be the silliest slave who ever lived." She saw the woman's mystified expression. "To run away in the face of an invasion of enemy troops when one could remain safely beneath the roof of one of Cyrene's richest and most powerful citizens..." She let her voice trail away artistically, and felt like taking a bow when she saw realization dawn on many faces.

"But if she didn't run away—" someone said.

The housewife interrupted. "You mean the slave might have been stolen? And her child is missing, too, that would only make her more valuable as proven brood stock." Her eyes brightened. "Laurus has enemies who would love to make him look foolish in the city's eyes. I wonder if Antikles might have—" She turned to her neighbor to share this juicy tidbit of speculation and the crowd was almost instantly abuzz. It appeared that Antikles, whoever he was, and Laurus had something of a history.

Tetisheri, her work done, slid unobtrusively into the crowd. Both Owls joined her shortly. "Neatly done, lady," Babak said, and Agape regarded her with something perilously close to respect.

"We passed a stall I'd like a closer look at," she said, and led them to a booth crammed with bolts of fabric. The vendor was a tall, thin woman with skin the color of ebony, and hair and body wrapped in lengths of fabric woven in intricate patterns brilliantly dyed. She claimed to be Mandinka from Kissi itself, and from the quality of her merchandise Tetisheri was inclined to believe her. Wherever she was from, her goods wouldn't last an hour in the Emporeum in Alexandria. Tetisheri bought out the Mandinka's stock there and then and sent Babak to fetch crewmen from the *Hapi II* to carry it back and stow it in the hold.

"Now then." She smiled at the Owls. "Let's go find out what new horrors Uncle Neb has in store for us."

Babak groaned and Agape rolled her eyes. When they got back they found Is and Dub drawn up before Neb, attired in House Nebenteru livery, dark blue tunics the color of the Middle Sea, with the badge of the sailing ship on their shoulders. They wore matching expressions of long-suffering patience as Neb paraded up and down before them, shoulders squared, hands clasped behind his back. He looked like he should be leading Caesar's forces. "Be tactful. Be discreet. Keep your eyes on me and Tetisheri. If we see someone misbehaving we will signal you. Just appearing and offering to help oftentimes calms people down."

"So does pitching them out on their behinds," Is said beneath his breath.

Babak giggled, and Nebenteru turned. "There you are, and about time, too! Get upstairs and into the proper attire, and then come down here so I can have a look at you."

There was no ignoring that peremptory tone so upstairs they went. Tetisheri wore her blue tunic again, this time with a collar, bracelets, and belt made of peridots and gold beads, an advertisement of the quality of Sea to Sea Imports' luxury goods in themselves. She brushed out her hair and draped a green palla she had bought in the marketplace the day before around her shoulders. Her sandals were delicate straps of leather dyed a darker green. She surveyed herself in the mirror and thought Keren would have approved. Maybe even Bast, too.

She went into the parlor to find Babak and Agape there before her. Their tunics, like Is and Dub's, were Nebenteru blue, so deep a blue the cloth seemed to have been dyed with crushed lapis, and they wore their House Nebenteru badges on their left shoulders with pride. Their hands and faces were clean, their hair neatly brushed, and in spite of all the previous heavy lifting they had been drafted into they both looked excited at the prospect of the afternoon and evening before them. She cleared a momentary obstruction from her throat and said, "Acceptable."

Babak looked crushed and Agape outraged, and Tetisheri laughed out loud. She waved a hand. "Off with you, to see what Uncle Neb has to say."

If two constituted a stampede then they stampeded down the stairs. She waited for their footsteps to die away before she knocked gently at their door. "It's Tetisheri. May I come in?" She didn't wait for an answer.

Urania and her daughter were crouched in the corner behind the door. Urania rose, pushing her child behind her, as Tetisheri closed the door and spoke softly. "You have nothing to fear from me, Urania."

Urania stared for a moment, and then grimaced. "Habit. My apologies, lady."

"None necessary. Let us sit."

Urania sat stiffly on one of the beds, her child next to her, watching Tetisheri with wide eyes. She really was lovely. In any room they were in, aunt, mother and child would have drawn all eyes, and deservedly so.

Tetisheri gestured. "I brought you both a palla in House Nebenteru colors."

Urania looked at the bundle sitting next to Tetisheri.

"You will leave the inn this evening. I don't know exactly when, but I'll send Agape or Babak for you. Please put these pallas on, obscuring as much of your features as you can." She smiled. "And still be able to see where you're going."

"Where are we going?"

"To our ship. It's nearby. We will be leaving Cyrene, bound for Alexandria, tomorrow morning at first light."

Urania was very still but her tension must have been great because her child gave a muffled protest. The arm around her shoulders loosened at once. "I'm sorry, my darling." She looked down as the girl looked up. "How would you like to meet your aunt?"

"Auntie Pipi?" The girl's face lit up. "Will she teach me how to pick the olives and stomp the grapes and mend the nets?"

There was a momentary silence when both women looked at the child, broken when Tetisheri stood up, making a production of shaking out and smoothing her tunic so that it fell just so over her sandals. "Be ready," she said to a point over Urania's head.

"We will be."

An hour later, the first inquisitive guest arrived. In two hours, the Waterfront Inn was even more crowded than the street outside. In three hours, the sun had begun to set and Neb caused the candelabra to be lit. He'd had them placed out of the draft caused by having all the doors and windows open to the air. With so many bodies crammed inside the room needed the ventilation.

Servers in spotless white tunics circulated with food and drink. The musicians played softly from their dais. Many of the guests were tradesmen and their spouses but there were also quite a few of the upper class in attendance. Everyone was dressed in their finest stolas and pallas and tunics and togas, and was wearing most of the jewelry usually stored in their strongboxes. Two women even sported diadems. There were Roman patricians, Greek scholars, Numidian nobles, Cyrenecian artists, and at least one courtier from Juba's court, who was accompanied by one Sextus Pompey, looking none the worse for wear after his dissipations of two nights' past. "Ah, youth," Dub said in Tetisheri's ear. "I don't recognize anyone else, do you?"

"No, thank all the gods that may be. Laurus isn't here, either."

"No loss." Dub strolled off to beguile a beautiful young matron whose older husband had deserted her in favor of *The Iliad* and *The Odyssey*.

Neb was flirting with every woman present over the age of consent, at the same time contriving not to offend their husbands and brothers. Tetisheri moved from one display to another, detailing each item, giving provenance where she knew it, calling in Uncle Neb when she didn't. As usual the Romans were most interested in anything pharaonic, because citizens of a political entity mere hundreds of years old would always and ever be sheepishly in awe (not to mention acquisitive) in the presence of the artifacts of another that went back thousands. She and Neb dealt only in the authentic, but less unscrupulous vendors could sell a Roman tourist anything with a snake on its brow, with a provenance—should it be examined too closely, which it never was—of mere days.

As the sun was setting Cornelia Metella came in the door, attended by the maidservant Tetisheri remembered seeing at her house. She went forward at once and bowed. "Cornelia Metella. You honor us with your presence."

"As I was honored by your invitation. May I be introduced to your uncle, the esteemed Nebenteru?"

"He will be delighted." She looked at the maid. "We

have a room and refreshments set aside for those servants accompanying our guests."

"How kind. Marcella?"

Tetisheri looked around and found Agape. The girl presented herself to Cornelia with hand to heart, lips, and brow, and led Marcella away.

"Now, my uncle. Ah, there he is."

They moved through the throng, Cornelia creating a path for them with a nod here and a smile there. It was like magic. "Uncle. Allow me to introduce you to the lady Cornelia Metella of Rome, visiting here in Cyrene."

Nebenteru took Cornelia's hand and kissed it. "I am so happy you were able to attend, lady. Come, let us find you some refreshment. And then perhaps I may show you some of my treasures?"

"Your exquisite taste is known across the Middle Sea, good Nebenteru. I look forward to seeing them all."

Uncle Neb very nearly purred, the pearl at the tip of his beard quivering in anticipation. He drew Cornelia's hand to his wrist and with a bow led her away.

Across the room Sextus was pointedly ignoring his stepmother.

"Mannerless young pup," Is said. "I'd take a stick to him." There was movement at the door and Is looked around. "What the—"

Tetisheri watched him cross the room to greet a soldier who had just come in, backed by two others. All three were in full armor from greaves to lorica to helmet, their bulk filling the open doorway from side to side. The armor was similar to a Roman legionnaire's but different enough in cut and color to distinguish one from the other. Useful on the battlefield and from their expressions they looked as if they were on their way to one. The man slightly in the lead wore the insignia of an optio, the two behind him serving men.

Is seemed to know the optio. After a brief conversation he turned to look around the room, and then led him straight to the courtier. The soldier saluted. The courtier responded, his face a mask. The soldier spoke, keeping his voice low.

Conversations became muted as all eyes turned to the two of them, the optio obviously making a report, the courtier taking it very seriously. Everyone strained to hear but both men were being discreet. The soldier saluted again and effaced himself. Is followed him to the door, where they spoke for a moment more, and exchanged a long handclasp.

Tetisheri looked at Dub, standing a little way away. He met her eyes and gave a slight nod. By the time she looked back at the door the soldiers had vanished and Is was coming towards her. She looked at the courtier, who was taking apologetic leave of his companions. The woman Tetisheri supposed was his wife looked white and strained in the candlelight, but she did manage a smile that was more than a grimace and not to cling to his hands. He bowed his head and turned to go. Sextus Pompey followed him as far as the door, and then looked over his shoulder, meeting Cornelia's gaze. Cornelia was looking at him with a face so devoid of expression she looked like the bust of Hera she and Neb had been admiring. Sextus came back into the room and stopped in front of her. "Goodbye, Mother."

"Take care, my son," she said.

He bowed over her hand and followed the courtier out the door and into the night.

"Not quite 'With your shield or on it,'" Dub said.

"Would you rather she shriek and tear her hair?"

Dub looked at Tetisheri, surprised. But then he was a man. He had been a soldier and had marched off to his share of battles, leaving the women and children behind, waiting.

"Caesar has landed," Is said from behind them.

"You don't say," Tetisheri said.

"Pastor says he has fewer than three thousand legionnaires with him and only a hundred and fifty cavalry. His ships ran into bad weather out of Sicily. It is the best chance Scipio and Juba will have to crush him with their superior force."

Cotta's words echoed in her ears. *I'm afraid the more pressing problem is feeding the ones we have.*

There would never be a better time, with everyone distracted by the news. No doubt it was spreading into the streets, panicking the populace. She went to Neb and Cornelia. "Uncle, you did say you wanted to show the *Hapi II* to our guests." To Cornelia, she said, "She's a lovely ship, if I say it who shouldn't. Would you like to see her?"

Cornelia, her face still a mask, took a moment to return from whatever cold, dark place she had gone to in her mind. Such was her control that her smile appeared less forced than those of the other women in the room. "That sounds a lovely idea, lady." She turned to Neb and smiled again, more naturally this time.

"Allow me to fetch your maid," Tetisheri said, and went swiftly from the room, signaling to Agape. "Get them," she said, and the girl ran for the stairs.

Tetisheri looked into the room set aside for the help and beckoned to Marcella, who rose so promptly to her feet that it was obvious she had only been waiting on word.

"It is true what they're saying, lady? That Caesar has landed in Africa?"

"I believe so." She turned her back on the resulting murmur and led Cornelia's servant into the hall as Agape came down the stairs. Only a single figure followed her, and Tetisheri saw that Urania had again bound the child to her breast and had used both pallas to smother the result. The extra bulk made her look fat and slow, and she stooped, which made her look old. No one who was seeking an escaped slave with her child would give this apparition a second glance.

Tetisheri barely had time to admire Urania's ingenuity and hope the two of them didn't suffocate before they gained the *Hapi II*. By the time they returned to the great room Neb had collected a group of sightseers, all eager to see this new ship of which they had heard so much. The merchants in particular were interested in estimating its tonnage. Tetisheri caught Neb's eye and gave him a slight nod. "Well then," he said heartily. "Please, allow me to introduce you to my darling. Lady?"

Cornelia again laid her fingers on his wrist and the two of them led the way, followed by the crowd. The servants trailed along behind.

"Show them to the room in the bow," Tetisheri whispered. "Jerome knows."

"Yes, lady." Agape followed.

Through the door she could hear a rising hum of activity, and see sails being shaken out on the warships.

"Lady." Babak tugged at her palla.

"What is it?"

"You're wanted." He led her around the stairs and out

ABDUCTION OF A SLAVE

a door that led into the back yard, which contained the kitchen gardens, the ovens, and the necessaries.

Where Apollodorus stood, waiting.

She was in his arms between one step and the next, kissing him, holding him, loving him.

"Caesar has landed," he said.

"I know. One of Juba's courtiers was here tonight and was brought the news. Is it true he has only three thousand legionnaires?"

"Yes. Juba and Scipio sail at once."

"And Juba's personal guard sails with them."

"Yes."

"Will you fight with them?"

He didn't answer.

She pulled back to look at him, trying to discern his beloved features through the dark of the night. "I haven't once seen you in the light, here in Cyrene."

"Nor I you." His big hands came up to her shoulders, warm and hard. "I love you, Tetisheri. With every part and fiber of my being, I love you."

"Please don't die."

It surprised a laugh out of him. A short one, but a laugh nonetheless.

He kissed her again, and then he was gone.

She stood where she was for long moments, weeping in silence, the breath shuddering out of her.

And then she wiped her face on her palla and turned around to return to the house.

Where she ran straight into Aurelius Cotta.

"Lady."

With an effort she got her heartbeat and her breath back

under control. "Do you know what I most loathe about you, Cotta?"

He sounded amused. "I await your answer with great anticipation."

"Your ubiquity."

He laughed.

The farewell from Apollodorus had shaken free her usual restraints. "Almost as much as I loathe your finding everything I say or do so thrice damned amusing!"

Still amused, he said, "Hadrumetum."

"Hadru what?"

"Hadrumetum. That is the port where you land on your return. Here." He handed her a scroll. "A letter directing any and every Roman warship you may encounter to grant you safe passage, signed by Caesar himself."

He stepped back and threw her a half-mocking salute. "Till Hadrumetum, lady."

14

They cast off before Ra peeped an eye over the eastern horizon. Neb watched as the stretch of water between the dock and the *Hapi II*'s hull widened. He looked sad, and, worst of all, bereft. Tetisheri wondered when he had last been anywhere he didn't have a ship waiting to set sail at his command. She kissed her fingertips to him. He returned the gesture, and with a resolute attitude that came close to breaking her heart turned and left before he had to watch them out of sight. He was followed by Is. Agape and Babak sailed with Tetisheri and would remain behind when next she left Alexandria.

There had been a brisk and almost bitter argument over who would accompany Tetisheri on this voyage. Is and Dub said both of them should come. So did Nebenteru, most vociferously of all. "The queen told you to take us with you," Dub pointed out.

Tetisheri was in no mood to parse Cleopatra's orders. "Do I really have to pull out the Eye?"

Dub sighed and produced a pair of dice. He and Is rolled three times. According to some arcane formula known only to them, Is lost and Dub was on board the *Hapi II* bound for Alexandria. Uncle Neb had been furious but Tetisheri watched that cranky little satyr follow Neb up the gangway and could feel nothing but relief that he had someone so able at his back.

She turned to face identical accusatory expressions from Babak and Agape. She raised a minatory finger. "You are going home, and you are staying there."

"Lady—"

"Did you hear what I said?"

Agape, who heard the flash of temper in the lady's voice, elbowed Babak in the side and he subsided.

They both sulked all the way back to Alexandria, though.

What was that she had said to herself about intelligent servants?

A strong westerly wind caught the sail as soon as they were outside the harbor. Nevertheless, on Tetisheri's instructions Jerome had all hands to the oars and the *Hapi II* took to her heels. The coastline of northern Africa passed them by as if Nut were winding a crank that was turning the earth beneath the hull, speeding them on their way home.

"How soon till we make port?" Tetisheri said, shading her eyes against the sun on the second morning at sea.

Jerome squinted at the coast, peered at their wake, and examined all horizons. "If Zephyrus continues to hold us in his hand, lady, two days. Possibly three. We're lucky we missed the storm that caught Caesar." He glanced at her. "I assume you want the men at the oars day and night."

"Tell them it means double pay." She caught herself. "I don't want them to drop in their seats, Jerome. Rotate them out every four hours or so."

"Teach your grandmother how to make dolmas." A pause. "Lady."

She was forced to smile. "My apologies. Double pay for you and the sailmaster, too, in case I didn't say. Our four guests do well?"

"Two of them have been sick since we left port. Otherwise, they're fine."

Sick or not, they would remain in the secret room in the bow. She trusted their crew but the fewer eyes on their guests the better.

In the event, it was two and one half days between pulling in their lines at Cyrene before throwing them out again in Alexandria, putting them into port when Ra was at his highest in the sky. They made directly to the Royal Harbor and at Tetisheri's direction moored directly behind the *Nut*. Only one crew member was on board but he recognized Tetisheri and waved off the guards that came at a trot.

Tetisheri turned to Jerome. "A fresh crew, immediately, and a fresh captain, too, if you think it necessary."

Jerome was outraged at the very thought. "Lady! The *Hapi II* is my ship! She does not sail without me!"

"What was I thinking. Very well." She turned to Dub. "Find the next ship sailing for Rome. One with decent quarters for passengers, if possible."

"Cornelia and her maid?"

"Yes." She looked at the palace. "Find a ship, pay for passage, but don't move Cornelia to it yet."

"Time to report in?"

She ignored Dub's raised eyebrow. "Go."

"Gone." He vaulted the railing and moved swiftly up the slip.

She went below to the room in the bow so cleverly concealed it would pass most inspections as a bulkhead. She pressed the hidden latch. As the door opened she was struck in the face with an odor of vomit and general misery. She held a fold of palla to her nose and spoke through it. "Ladies."

Nausea had not dared to strike so august a personage as Cornelia Metella. She rose to her feet. "We have reached Alexandria?"

"Yes. My apologies, but I must ask you to remain below for a little longer. We are arranging passage for you and your maid to Rome. That is still your wish?"

"It is."

"I go now to make my report." She let her eyes flick toward Urania and her daughter and saw that Cornelia understood no mention would be made in front of them of who Tetisheri's employer was. "Urania, I will return shortly with transportation. Do you need anything?"

Urania shook her head. It looked as if she and Cornelia's maid had borne the brunt of the seasickness.

"I'll have someone bring you fresh water and some dry biscuit. I promise you," she said when she saw the expression on Urania's face, "it will help."

She closed the door behind her and went to find Jerome, who promised he himself would deliver food and water to their guests. "Thank you. I must go ashore for an hour, no more. In the meantime, prepare to accept cargo. Grain, oil, other foodstuffs. As much as the *Hapi II* can carry and keep above the water line."

His eyebrows went up. "Where are we taking it?"

"Back to Cyrenaica."

He made a face. "Scipio?"

"Caesar."

"Oh, well, then."

She went away, shaking her head. Outnumbered three to one, everyone was still betting on Caesar.

For that matter, so was she.

She gained the docks and made her way as fast as she could to the side door she always used, where she found Charmion already waiting for her. "You saw us come in?"

"No, but she did."

Of course she had.

A brisk walk through the halls delivered them to one of the smaller receiving chambers. Cleopatra was seated on a small throne placed on a dais one step up from the floor. Several advisors attended her, including Sosigenes and the High Priest of Isis and a Roman functionary she didn't know. The queen wasn't in full regalia but she did wear the cobra on her brow. This was official, then. Notes would be taken. Tetisheri's report would be discussed.

Charmion moved to one side and Tetisheri walked forward until she was the appropriate distance from her sovereign and went to her knees, bowing deeply.

"We see our subject, Tetisheri of House Nebenteru. Our heart is gladdened by her return home to Alexandria. Rise."

Tetisheri stood, hands folded, eyes lowered, waiting. In this company she would not speak until she was bidden.

"Report."

Tetisheri raised her head. "Majesty. I am come from Cyrene these two and a half days past with the news that Caesar has landed his forces at Hadrumetum."

From the corner of her eye she saw the Roman start. Sosigenes and the High Priest were made of sterner stuff, maintaining their stoic expressions.

There was a moment's silence.

"So," Cleopatra said. "And what else?"

Tetisheri fixed her gaze at some point over Cleopatra's left shoulder. "Majesty, I have it from a reputable source—" she might have stressed "reputable" because she saw Cleopatra's eyes widen just a trifle "—that a storm scattered Caesar's ships between Sicily and Africa. The forces he landed are much fewer in number than those fielded by Scipio and Juba. When I left Cyrene Scipio and Juba were mustering their forces and preparing to sail out to meet him."

Another weighty silence. "How many fewer?"

Tetisheri now knew the feeling of every courtier who brought unwanted news to her queen. Best to get it over with quickly. "Three to one."

The High Priest continued to look like a wildebeest stuffed and mounted on some nomarch's walls, minus the horns. Sosigenes looked distant, as if he were calculating the dimensions of Caesar's impending defeat. The Roman looked perfectly appalled.

"Well," Cleopatra said at length. "This is news indeed. We thank you, Tetisheri, for bringing it to us so speedily."

It was clearly a dismissal. Tetisheri bowed and backed

away far enough to where she could pass through the door Charmion was holding open for her. "There is more," she told her when they were both safely on the other side of it.

"No. Really?"

Tetisheri followed Charmion again through various hallways and passages until they came to Cleopatra's private rooms, where she was shown into the small parlor, the one with the balcony overlooking the Royal Harbor. The room was empty as yet and she crossed to the balcony. There was *Hapi II*, riding the royal slip opposite the *Nut* as if she had every right to be there.

"She's lovely, Sheri, truly."

"And she sails as if she has wings."

"She had need of it, this voyage."

"She did indeed." Tetisheri turned. Cleopatra had stripped off her jewels and the royal cobra. Her hair was a little ruffled and she looked altogether more human than she had sitting on that throne a few minutes before. Tetisheri smiled. "Welcome back."

Cleopatra chuckled and rubbed her scalp. "I swear before Isis, that snake is heavier than both crowns."

"Yes, yes, it's so awful being queen."

"Such disrespect! Out with your tongue." Behind them Iras came with a tray. Cleopatra waited until the door closed behind her to put her hands on Tetisheri's shoulders. She looked deep into the blue eyes. "Yes, I thought so. My poor dear. Sit down. We will have tea, and honey cakes, and you can tell me the rest."

She led Tetisheri to a chair soft with cushions and sat her down. A steaming cup of tea found its way into her hands, all while Tetisheri struggled to regain her composure.

The tea, some concoction of Cleopatra's own, no doubt, was soothing. Tetisheri let her head fall back against the cushions, feeling the tension in her body easing. "Why did you have me report before witnesses?"

"I was to meet with them to discuss something I can't even remember now. The *Hapi II* won't be the only boat into the harbor today bearing this news. Better those three hear it with me than a garbled version from the waterfront."

"Who was the Roman?"

A snort. "That idiot? Manlius. One of the Scipiones, and a more useless bunch of lickspittles and hangers-on I have yet to meet. He came bearing Cotta's regrets, who was unable to attend due to some slight illness."

Tetisheri raised her head. "Cotta was unable to attend because he is presently in Cyrene."

"Ah." The queen was silent for a moment. "I knew he was gone and wherever Scipio was seemed the most likely place, but it's good to have it confirmed. Tell me. Tell me all, beginning to end."

Tetisheri told it all, or almost all, from the moment they had stepped ashore in Cyrene until the moment the *Hapi II* had set sail for home.

Cleopatra sat frowning over her tea. "So Cornelia is still on board?"

"Yes. With her maid. I have Dub looking for passage to Rome for the both of them. She says it's what she wants."

Cleopatra waved a hand. "No need." She raised her voice. "Charmion?"

The door opened. "My queen?"

"Send for Markos."

"At once, Majesty."

The door closed and Tetisheri raised her eyebrows. "You're sending her home on the *Nut*?"

"If even half of what you say is true, she will welcome the courtesy. If Sextus manages to get himself killed in the upcoming battle, she'd much rather hear the news at home, surrounded by family and friends."

"She seems to have a pretty good friend right here in Alexandria."

Cleopatra smiled. "Now. To your requirements. Charmion?"

Door, opening. "Majesty?"

"Send for Horemheb."

"At once, Majesty." Door, closing. "I will tell Horemheb to begin loading the *Hapi II* immediately. And you may tell Aurelius Cotta—" she made his name sound like a curse, which Tetisheri understandably found delightfully appropriate "—that I shall begin loading those ships presently in harbor and sending them after you."

"He'll be overjoyed."

Cleopatra showed her teeth. "I don't doubt it. He knew I would do exactly that when you reported in."

Tetisheri thought about it for a moment. "You mean he never meant to hold me hostage to Neb returning with supplies."

"A sly and wily character, our Cotta. He knows as well as I do that a threat to loved ones is a better inducement even than money. You may also tell Aurelius Cotta from me that I have urgent need of the aid and counsel of my subject, Nebenteru, head of House Nebenteru, who carries my favor and my esteem."

"That is a message I will take great joy in delivering, O most high."

Cleopatra grinned. "Entirely my pleasure." She bent forward and refilled their cups. "All right," she said. "Tell me about Apollodorus."

Tetisheri raised startled eyes. "How did you—"

"Oh, please." Cleopatra waved a dismissive hand. "I knew he was in Cyrene because I sent him there. I knew he would hear of your coming. I knew he would find a way to see you."

"He's in Juba's palace guard." Tetisheri hadn't meant it to come out like an accusation, but there they were. "He sailed with Juba three nights ago."

Cleopatra stared at her. "He what? Tetisheri, by Isis and Osiris, that was not part of his remit. I didn't ask him to put himself in a position to fight beside Juba, of all people!"

"No, but you probably told him to get as close to Juba as he could."

"Yes." A deep sigh. "Yes, I did do that."

"If he is hurt—if he is—"

"Stop. Stop right there. Don't borrow trouble, Tetisheri. Remember who he his. Remember who his father was."

The trouble was, she did. Vividly. So did too many others. "It will take the afternoon at least to load the *Hapi II*. I'm going home, to spend a night in my own bed." Alone, she thought, and could see that Cleopatra could read that thought in her eyes.

When Cleopatra spoke, it was in a very soft voice. "It is the bane of my existence, Sheri, that my commands send my friends into danger." She, too, rose to her feet and met Tetisheri's eyes, with sympathy but also with determination.

"My only consolation is that they do it not for me, but for Egypt."

A memory came to Tetisheri, of Apollodorus telling her very nearly the same thing in almost the same words. She bent her head. "We know that, Pati. And we do it gladly."

Well. Perhaps not gladly. But they could see and appreciate the necessity. And Alexandria was Tetisheri's home, too. In a small way in her role as the Eye of Isis her duty was to defend it, every bit as much as Cleopatra's duty was in hers. "One thing, Pati." She hesitated. "I have a favor to ask."

Cleopatra raised her brows. "Ask."

Tetisheri took a deep breath. "Writs of citizenship for two people, a mother and a daughter. And no questions asked."

Cleopatra gave her a long, steady look. "Done. I will tell Horemheb to issue the papers at your request."

As simple as that, and as complicated. This wasn't just a favor for a friend. This was recompense due for a job of work, and reward for that job well done. Cleopatra proved it by saying, "My thanks again for bringing the news so quickly, Sheri. The last letter I had from Caesar was from Sicily, when he was about to set sail. It is well to know these things in advance, so as to be able to calm a population prone to panic at the sight of a raised banner."

"Remind them all the action is taking place three hundred leagues to the west. That should calm them down." They smiled at each other. "Do you want to see Cornelia?"

"Yes. I will come down with you. Charmion!"

Door, opening. "Majesty?"

"My cloak, and a guard. I wish to walk down to the port."

"Majesty."

Charmion, intuiting that this was not something to which Cleopatra wanted attention drawn, summoned a guard of four, no more. Thus insulated against assassination, they walked out into the sun and down the steps to the dock where the *Nut* and the *Hapi II* bobbed. Markos was just stepping onto the *Nut* when he saw Cleopatra. He paused and bowed. "Majesty."

"Markos." Cleopatra stopped, looking over his command. "You've sent for your crew?"

"I have, Majesty."

"She looks ready, your *Nut*."

He smiled slowly. "We are always ready, Majesty. We never know when you will set us a task, and it is our goal never to let you down." He looked over her shoulder. "Or who you will send with us. Lady." He bowed slightly to Tetisheri.

"Oh, not Tetisheri this time, Markos. Another friend. Tetisheri?"

"Majesty." Tetisheri boarded the *Hapi II* and went below, emerging a few moments later with Cornelia Metella and her maid. The maid knelt. Cornelia bowed, very low.

"Cornelia Metella." Cleopatra came forward, her hands outstretched, and raised up Cornelia. "It has been too long since we have met."

"It has, Majesty. You have not changed."

"Nonsense! I'm a mother now."

"I heard. Congratulations."

They looked at each other and smiled. Cornelia said, "I am grateful to be removed from a situation that had become, shall we say, uncomfortable. Thank you for that."

"Rather thank my Eye, who saw your need and met it."

Both women smiled at Tetisheri, who tried not to squirm. "My queen's wishes are my own, lady."

Cleopatra snorted, and Cornelia might have laughed if she stood less on her dignity. Cleopatra gestured toward Markos. "Allow me to introduce you to Markos, captain of the vessel *Nut*. I have commanded him to take you home."

For the first time since she'd met her, Tetisheri had the glorious experience of seeing Cornelia Metella taken aback. "I—I—how can I thank you, Majesty. You do me too much honor."

"Not at all, Cornelia Metella. You were kind to a young girl adrift in a society foreign to her. You saved me from many pitfalls and contretemps." Cleopatra grinned. "When I think of you, I think of those two young men who cornered me in—whose garden was it? Your father's? Cato's?"

"Cato's, Majesty."

"Cato never did like me."

"Cato doesn't like anyone, Majesty, especially when they wear a crown."

Cleopatra chuckled. "True enough. Well. Given your recent experiences in Cyrene, I expect you can't wait to get home. Although I would happily have you guest here with me as long as you liked."

A faint sigh. "I do long for my own bed, Majesty."

"I won't keep you, then. I know what it is to be too long away from home. I…" She hesitated, but only for a moment. "I'm sorry not to see Sextus with you."

"At least I was able to say goodbye to him." Cornelia looked bleak. "Which makes me one of the lucky ones. Many mothers will not be able to say the same."

For the first time Tetisheri thought that Cornelia's care

for her stepson might be more than simply a last duty to her dead husband.

Cleopatra bowed her head in acknowledgement of this painful truth. Caesarion wasn't six months old but she could see the day she was in Cornelia's sandals, and she could sympathize. "Markos, sail as soon as the crew is on board and supplies are loaded."

Markos nodded. "Majesty." He looked at Cornelia. "Where are we going, lady?"

"Ostia. How long will it take?"

He did as Jerome had, squinted at the sky, the clouds, the water, tested the wind with a wet forefinger. "Three days, I should think. Four at most."

She nodded and looked at Cleopatra. "Again, Majesty, I—"

Cleopatra raised a hand. "Peace. It is my very great pleasure to be able to do this small thing for you. Know you are welcome in Alexandria anytime. Till we meet again, Cornelia Metella."

"Till then, Majesty."

Tetisheri walked Cleopatra back to the palace. At the door she said, out of earshot of the guard, "When you go to Rome, it will be as well to have friends there."

Cleopatra smiled at her, and passed inside without answering.

And it cost nothing to be kind, Tetisheri thought, watching the door close behind her.

Tetisheri saw Cornelia and her maid onto the *Nut*, watching as the two women found seats in the small cabin on the aft deck.

The last time Tetisheri had occupied that same cabin, she had been with Apollodorus.

Dub returned with passage for two on a freighter bound for Rome by way of Syrakousai, and swore roundly when she told him they weren't needed after all. "And, Dub, we leave in the morning."

He cocked his head. "Back to Cyrene?"

"Yes. Cargo is being commandeered from the royal warehouses as we speak." She hesitated. "I need your escort this evening, if you would be so kind?"

He laughed. "Much as my life is worth to refuse you that or anything, Sheri. I'm going to go get some food."

"Get enough for four."

The *Nut*'s crew appeared with a cart full of supplies. They were loaded and without ado the *Nut*'s crew cast off. The square sail caught enough of the last of the day breeze to carry them out of the harbor. The oars came out, Tetisheri heard the sailmaster call the count to a rhythmic splash, and the small ship vanished into the dusk. Above them the Pharos flashed, a beacon in the night.

"Nicely done," Dub said from behind her, making her jump. He held out a bundle tied up in a piece of threadbare cotton. "Rolls with meat and beans, and—" he held up a small amphora "—watered wine."

"Good man."

She went below and brought Urania and her daughter on deck, who, if disheveled from the days spent below, looked all the better for the fresh air. "Keep your pallas around you still, and walk behind me as servants do."

"Are we not safe in Alexandria, lady?"

"An escaped slave, if she is known as such, is safe nowhere in the Middle Sea, and you know it."

"Yes, lady."

Tetisheri touched her shoulder. "I'm sorry, Urania. But we must be careful, until we can establish identities for you here. I will say that that is in hand. Then you will be safe." She smiled at the child, who stared unblinkingly back. Tetisheri had spoken too many harsh words to her mother.

They sat on deck in the shade of the boom, eating and drinking until it was truly dark, after which they walked up Lochias to the Queen's Guard encampment. Dub waved down a cabrio, which disgorged a rowdy quartet of soldiers returning from leave who were only discouraged from accosting the women by Dub meaningfully tapping the hilt of his gladius. Amazing how any one of the Five Soldiers could project threat at a mere gesture. She wondered if they taught a class in it at the gymnasium.

They boarded the cabrio and took it down Lochias to the house opposite the Promenade. Dub waited in the cabrio as Tetisheri ushered them up the walk and knocked on the door, praying that Calliope was home that evening. Phryne answered the door, looking her usual forbidding self. "The lady Tetisheri to see the lady Calliope. It is urgent."

Phryne looked from her to the two figures behind her.

"Yes, I have my maids with me. Would you like me to send them round the back?"

Phryne must have been in her mistress' confidence because she allowed them entrance without question. "Into the small parlor with you." The room was not nearly as well furnished as the parlor with which Tetisheri was most familiar. That room must already be occupied. By whom, she wondered without much interest.

After a little while they heard footsteps and a male voice, grumbling. A female voice, coaxing. The front door opened and, what felt like at long last, closed again. A few moments' wait, and then footsteps came toward them in a stumbling run. The door swung back with a bang—luckily no priceless work of art was hanging on that part of the wall—and Calliope entered so hastily she nearly fell forward. She caught herself. "Lady?" she said sharply. "Phryne said—Phryne said—"

Urania stood up and let the palla slip to the floor. "Pipi?"

For a moment Calliope could only gape, and then she came forward with hesitant steps. "Ranny? Ranny, is it really you? Ranny? Ranny!"

This last was nearly a shriek. The two women fell into each other's arms, sobbing. Tetisheri went to the door. Behind her she heard Urania say in a tear-soaked voice, "This is my daughter. Elphis, meet your Auntie Pipi."

"Hello, Elphis." Calliope's voice broke on the name. "Hello, my little love."

Phryne was waiting with the door open. She closed it behind Tetisheri, as taciturn as ever.

Fifteen minutes later Tetisheri was home and falling into the arms of her own family.

Absent Nebenteru.

And Apollodorus.

And the builders. Acacius must have torn his crew free from the culinary charms of Phoebe and Nebet at last.

Bast had warmed her bed. She fell into it and was instantly asleep.

The next morning Tetisheri again took leave of her household and found Keren waiting at the door, packed bag at her feet.

"What do you think you're doing?"

"I'm coming with you."

"No, you're not. Did you not hear me last night? War has come. Again. It's going to be bloody and dangerous. Again. You could get hurt."

One slim black eyebrow rose in polite interrogation. "And you are the only one of us who can choose to put themselves at risk for the greater good? I'm a doctor, Tetisheri. I can save lives." She nodded at the door. "Rhode is waiting. Shall we go?"

As promised Cotta was at Hadrumetum, with carts of every shape and description drawn by donkeys and mules and horses and oxen. There was even a string of camels that spat and bit and kicked everyone who came within reach but they could carry twice their own weight and more for leagues on a single drink of water. Cotta greeted Tetisheri and the heavy strongbox the queen had sent with positive relief. The sight of it certainly motivated the owners and drivers of the various animals in his supply train. The ship's hold was cleared and the carts and animals loaded before the sun set that evening.

Cotta stood on the deck of the *Hapi II*, watching his ill-matched caravan lumber slowly off with an expression of deep satisfaction and, although he tried to hide it, not a little relief. "Very well done, lady. We are currently feeding our horses on seaweed, and were it not for your timely arrival I fear the troops themselves would have been next. My compliments and Caesar's gratitude to your queen." His smile was charming.

She remained unmoved. "She offers you her compliments in return, and begs me to inform you that she is presently loading more ships with supplies for Caesar. Only a destination is needed."

He nodded, unsurprised at this news, as Cleopatra had foreseen. "Please tell her, with my thanks again and Caesar's as well, that Ruspina would best suit our purposes going forward." He paused. "To your knowledge, is Vitruvius still a scholar in residence at the Mouseion?"

"I believe so."

"Upon your return, could you find him and tell him Caesar needs him at Ruspina? And perhaps give him passage?"

"Certainly."

That single word was of a temperature to raise frost on a roaring fire and his grin was appreciative. It faded somewhat at her next words. "The queen also begs me to convey her wishes for the speedy return to her city of one of her most trusted and faithful citizens, Nebenteru, master trader and head of House Nebenteru. She finds herself in urgent need of his counsel."

He bowed slightly. "Who am I to gainsay the wishes of the Lady of the Two Lands?"

"One more thing." She waved Keren forward. "You may remember Keren, also of House Nebenteru. She is a doctor, Mouseion-trained. She has brought medical supplies, and offers her services to set up a clinic to treat your wounded."

Keren had kitted herself out in rough gray homespun, her black curls bound back out of the way. She nodded. "Aurelius Cotta."

"Doctor. You are more welcome here than all the supplies that came up out of the *Hapi II*'s hold."

"I will do my best by your wounded, sir." She looked over her shoulder. "Crixus is my assistant."

Crixus looked less Keren's assistant than her bodyguard. Armed with gladius and pugio, he obviously meant to.

Cotta's lips twitched. "On behalf of our casualties, I thank you both with all my heart."

Tetisheri stepped toward him and spoke in a voice meant only for his ears. "You will create a safe environment for her to treat your soldiers, Cotta, or your own life will be forfeit."

There was no smile or laugh this time. "Understood, lady. My life for hers."

"A price I am glad you are willing to pay."

Keren gave Tetisheri an exasperated glance and accepted Cotta's hand in stepping to the dock. Crixus winked at Tetisheri and followed.

"Whoever is minding the store?" Dub said behind her.

"Castus, I expect."

He shuddered.

But when the *Hapi II* made landfall again at Cyrene, Uncle
Neb refused to return to Alexandria. "I met someone who
says he can guide me to where the silphium grows, or some
of it. I want to see with my own eyes what the problem is."

"Uncle," she said despairingly, "there are men at war
everywhere between here and Carthage. Armies are no
respecter of persons not in the armor of their own side.
Please come home with me. We can look for the silphium
later."

He was stern. "For shame, Tetisheri. That's not the trader
I know speaking." She was crushed, and let it show. He
softened. "For the moment you are tasked with carrying
supplies to the father of our queen's son and heir." He raised
a minatory finger. "Keep good counts of loads and trips, so
we may present an accurate bill for services rendered at the
end of this conflict."

She would not be diverted. "You're not staying here to
look for silphium. You're staying because you want to find
out who murdered Timur."

"That, too, my dear."

She looked at Is, who cast up his eyes and sighed. "I'll
stay with him."

She clasped Is's hand. "Thank you." She looked back at
Neb. "Something I meant to tell you before I left, Uncle.

You'll remember I delivered Cornelia's invitation to your party by hand."

"Yes?"

"I came back by way of Timur's house." She saw his gathering wrath and held up a hand, palm out. "I didn't go in. I didn't even stop. All we did was drive down to the end of the street and back."

"But?"

"I saw someone there. He was hiding at the back of the house but he wasn't careful and I saw him. So did Babak, and we both recognized him."

"Who was he?"

"He was the optio who came for Juba's officer the evening of your party." She looked at Is. "You remember. You greeted him."

She couldn't read the expression on Is's face, but he answered naturally. "Yes. Dub and I met him in our rambles around the city." He hesitated, which in itself was odd. Is never hesitated. "You're sure it was him at Timur's house?"

She wondered at the plea she thought she heard in his voice. "Yes. Babak is, too."

Some trick of the light made Is appear older than his years. "His name is Pastor. He's a legionnaire, retired after Bibracte. Juba brought him and others like him out of retirement to train the new conscripts he's been yanking off farms all over Cyrenaica."

"You know him?"

Is sighed. "Yes." Something like sorrow crossed his face. "He shipped out with Juba and Scipio when word came of Caesar's landing." He saw the question in her eyes. "I asked at his tavern."

Tetisheri looked back at Uncle Neb. "Uncle, it could have been an attempted robbery that went too far. You said Timur was tortured. He was our factor. It's a lucrative position anywhere in the Middle Sea."

"His family wasn't there. Or at least there were no bodies."

"His family?"

"I told you. I've been asking questions. The more distance Juba puts between himself and his subjects, the freer they are with their tongues. Timur had three wives and seven children. I saw no sign of them. It looked like he knew someone was coming for him and he got his loved ones safely out of the way before they arrived."

"Why not leave with them?"

"That more than anything else leads me to believe he knew who was coming, and when, and why. Maybe his relationship with his murderers was such that he thought he could presume upon acquaintance, that he had friends among them who would cause the others to stay their hands." Neb shrugged. "But money always comes first. A thief forgets that at his peril, and so it proved with Timur." A deep sigh. "At any rate, I have a notion where he sent his family. It is some leagues outside the city, up the coast."

Tetisheri managed a smile. "And at the same time, you can look for silphium, so we'll have some answers for Judoc and the others."

His embrace was long enough for her to hide her face in his shoulder, lest he see the tears in her eyes. "Don't worry, Sheri. If I know anything about Caesar this will be over soon and we'll make plans to take out the *Hapi III* on her maiden voyage. This time to Ephesus, perhaps? Or even through the delta and up the river to Syrene." He gave her a hearty kiss and forced her on board.

He waited until the *Hapi II* was away from the slip before giving them a jaunty wave, and turned to go back up the gangway, trailed by Is. Neither of them looked very happy.

Tetisheri stayed at the railing, watching until both men were out of sight.

15

That was the first week of January.

For the next three months Tetisheri and the *Hapi
II* ferried supplies from Alexandria and Pelusium
and Paraetonium to Ruspina. The first cargo to Ruspina
included Vitruvius, attired in full armor and accompanied
by a set of tools in a massive wooden chest. The news they
took back to Alexandria was that there had been much
marching and skirmishing, but that Scipio had yet to force
Caesar into a face-to-face conflict. In part that was due to
the ill winds that had scattered Caesar's invasion fleet, which
was still dribbling into Africa one ship at a time. Cotta, in a
rare burst of candor, said that Caesar was waiting until all
his forces were assembled to act.

"Tchaa!" said the queen.

Zephyrus continued kind and the weather remained fair
and breezy. They were stopped twice by Roman warships,

but with writs of safe passage guaranteed by both Caesar and Cleopatra, in documents festooned with official-looking seals and ribbons, they were sent on their way without further question. Of pirates they saw no sign, as the men Rameses III had called the "Sea Peoples" had withdrawn to the east to stay out of harm's way. Caesar had once been kidnapped by Cilician pirates, had talked his way out of bondage, and had promptly returned with a fleet to capture and kill them all. They hadn't forgotten.

Come to think of it, the pirates would do well to withdraw in the other direction entirely and take shelter behind the Pillars of Hercules.

As the weeks went by they were joined by other, much slower traders and freighters and massive grain ships, flying flags from Carthage to Hispania to Judea to Cilicia to Athens to, of course, Rome, all riding low in the water beneath the weight of their cargoes. The *Hapi II*, laden or not, passed them as if they were standing still. Tetisheri grieved, just a little, that Neb wasn't there to enjoy it as much as she did.

Tetisheri's skin turned a deeper, ever more golden brown beneath Ra's constant and benevolent rays and fortunately Jerome kept her occupied with tasks about the boat so that she didn't have too much time to brood over Apollodorus. What time she did spend in thought was usually at night, staring up at the stars, so many, so bright, so various, so immortal. Thanks to Heliodoros, the astronomy professor at the Mouseion and a rigorous and exacting teacher, she could put a name to all twelve constellations, and could even find her way home by Ursa Minor if she had to.

So would the next Tetisheri, whether she lived a hundred or a thousand years after her. A humbling thought, and a comforting one. Beneath those glittering, diamond eyes, which some said were apertures through which the gods watched to weigh and judge them all, it was difficult to take seriously the woes of mankind. Most of which were self-inflicted.

As the stars revolved above her head, as the sail tugged at its lines, as the oars swished through the water, she reviewed everything that had happened since they had first come to Cyrene, and came to certain conclusions. She knew who killed Timur, and why. She knew who killed Fulvio, and why.

She couldn't prove it, and the war had decided for her that she would never have to. The deaths of the two men were as nothing to the conflict raging across North Africa, and she had no chance of bringing anyone to justice for anything. Cotta would never allow any investigation to go forth. Caesar couldn't afford it.

It was more profitable to worry about Apollodorus.

Which was to say, not profitable at all.

The second time they landed at Ruspina, the town had almost overnight acquired intimidating defenses in the form of ramparts where only a wall had been before, towers and fixed ballistae springing up like lethal weeds every twenty feet. Vitruvius had come down to the dock to receive yet another large chest full of who knew what deadly things his able imagination had in store for Scipio's forces.

"You've been busy," she said.

He followed her eyes to the new defenses and gave a satisfied nod. "And not to no purpose."

"How much is enough?" she said to him as the chest was being loaded onto a cart by four puffing legionnaires.

He looked at her, unsmiling, and she saw no trace of apology there. "We want this war over, lady."

"And you have to kill all of them to achieve that?"

He gave a brief shake of his head, still unsmiling. "We don't want the enemy pardoned so as to live so we have to fight them again. Which is what we have been doing. Enough."

"Vitruvius." She stopped and had to find her voice to begin again. "Many of them are legionnaires like yourselves."

"And many of us know many of them. But this time they chose the wrong side." A dry smile. "Some of the smarter ones know that already."

"Defections?"

"A steady trickle." The smile vanished. "And the more we kill, the more deserters will find their way to our lines."

A capable, even gifted man, justifying destruction in the service of creation, a quid pro quo, slaughter for peace. "Are any of Caesar's men deserting to join Scipio and Juba?"

He snorted. "None, lady."

There was no difficulty in believing that.

He looked at her and his expression softened, just a little. "Your compassion does you credit, lady. But we want an end to this war now, not later, not a year from now, with half or more of us casualties or dead. The Pompeiians refuse to admit defeat. So they must die, in numbers large enough that they will, finally, accept it."

She bent her head in acknowledgement. "What news may I take back to Alexandria?"

He shrugged. "Scipio fights a running battle, lady. Ambush and retreat, repeat. Caesar is busy locking every back door he can. Hadrumetum barricaded themselves against him, Leptis welcomed him, Ruspina—" He gestured over his shoulder. "As you see."

"There has been as yet no fixed battle?"

He shook his head. "There was a small one here. Labienus and Petreius led their forces. We were outnumbered and in the end bested, but our troops withdrew in good order."

She couldn't tell if this was true or what he wanted to believe, or what Caesar wanted them all to believe. "Word has come that Juba marches to join Scipio with four legions and a hundred war elephants."

"And his well-respected light cavalry, yes, we know." His expression lightened. "However, news has just come that Bocchus attacked Cyrenaica the moment after Juba marched. Juba's attention is now, ah, divided, shall we say."

Tetisheri was less concerned with Juba's distraction than she was with Bocchus' attack on a city from which Neb might now be waiting for her and the *Hapi II* to extricate him and Is. "Cyrene itself?"

He shook his head. "Bocchus's forces in no way match Juba's in number, strength, or experience. Juba left the city well protected. A useful diversion, only."

"Did Caesar…"

He looked puzzled for a moment and then his expression cleared as he took her meaning. "That's way above my pay grade, lady." He smiled and this time it looked real. "But we may certainly call it fortuitous."

Where was Apollodorus in all this? she thought as they cast off. Was he well? Hurt? At the front of the battle, or safely behind?

The knot of fear she had carried with her since their

leave-taking at the Waterfront Inn became even tighter. She wondered, too, where Neb and Is were, and how they fared.

And then, because she couldn't do anything else, she got back to work.

Cleopatra, when Tetisheri took the news back, did her excellent imitation of the Sphinx and made no comment, but if Bocchus had been bought, it was very probably done with Egyptian gold.

Cleopatra sent the *Hapi II* to Pelusium this time, loading grain from scows anchored in the delta. The Lady of the Two Lands had no wish to empty the grain warehouses in Alexandria in service of anyone, including Caesar. She had no problem insisting that the northern nomarchs empty theirs. They grumbled but complied, less reluctant than they might have been because the Nile had risen that summer for the first time in three years. Egyptians and Alexandrians alike tied the event to the birth of Caesarion, a rebirth of the ruling family and a rebirth of the country, complementary events obviously blessed by the gods for the good of all the land.

It could do Cleopatra's standing in the realm no harm. The first duty of any ruler and certainly the one most guaranteed to promote their longevity was to keep their people fed.

Vide Caesar's difficulties at present.

Although when she returned to Ruspina, she was greeted with the news that Caesar's forces had taken Sarsura with all of its granaries intact. A coup, one that would definitely sting Scipio, who was having his own problems feeding his troops. Surely this meant a change in fortune for Caesar.

"For the moment," Vitruvius said, who had made a habit of meeting the *Hapi II* when he saw it come into the harbor. "Until we run out of food again."

"Where is he now?"

"Skirmishing around Uzitta. One bit of unalleviated good news, though—Caesar has persuaded the Gaetuli to rebel against Juba."

The Gaetuli were a large but scattered tribe who lived from the Aures Mountains to the Atlas Mountains, clustering in fertile valleys and desert oases. They were combative and capable and for sale. By "persuaded" Vitruvius meant "bought," and, Tetisheri thought, like Bocchus, undoubtedly with Egyptian gold, very probably carried in the hold of the *Hapi II*.

He saw her expression and laughed. "Indeed, lady, in this endeavor we could not do without your services or your queen's goodwill."

They stood to one side as Jerome had the latest small, heavy chest brought ashore. Tetisheri handed a letter to Vitruvius, tied and sealed in three places. "Caesar, eyes only."

"As usual." He proffered one in return. "Cleopatra, eyes only."

"As usual." She looked toward the city, whose ramparts were now adorned with fixed ballistae every ten feet, and repeated herself. "Again, you have been busy."

"We have, and again, not to no purpose." He sounded as satisfied as he looked.

"Shall Caesar ever bring Scipio and Juba to the point?"

"I believe so, and soon."

"You sound confident."

"I am. More importantly, so is Caesar."

"Define soon."

"Two weeks, perhaps. No more. He has ordered a *lustratio* for tomorrow." He saw her expression and elaborated. "A ceremony of ritual purification. It always heartens, and hardens the men. He would not have done so had he not meant to finally force the issue."

She thought for a moment. "Scipio has waged a war of attrition."

"Yes."

"But Caesar knew that," she said slowly, and with a sudden realization added, "And waged one of his own."

He smiled at her. "We'll make a strategist of you yet, lady."

She sighed. "No wonder he keeps winning battles."

She took this news and Caesar's missive back to Alexandria. Cleopatra received her in her private salon and read it in her presence. "The matter will be resolved in two weeks, he says here."

"So says Vitruvius as well."

"Perhaps by the time you return."

"Or even before."

Cleopatra nodded. "Keren?"

"Well. Busy."

Cleopatra looked back at Caesar's letter, her face somber. "She'll be busier soon."

"Yes."

"Wait while I write a response."

This was quickly done, and when she handed it to Tetisheri she said, "Return by way of Cyrene this time, Sheri. Bocchus's forces never penetrated that far, and it would gladden my heart to hear word that Neb is well."

Tetisheri bent her head. "Majesty."

To Tetisheri's immense relief, Neb and Is were waiting for them dockside, packed bags and a few boxes of goods beside them. "We saw you when you rounded the point," Neb said. He swept Tetisheri up into a comprehensive hug. "No need to make you wait. And we're done here, anyway."

She emerged from the embrace with tears in her eyes and a huge smile on her face only to be caught and twirled in a circle by Is, which greeting was punctuated by a smacking kiss.

She spoke the thing first and foremost on her mind. "Apollodorus?"

Is's grin faded. "No word, Sheri."

Neb shook his head gravely.

She stiffened her spine and was proud when her voice was steady. "We're bound for Ruspina."

"What's our cargo?"

"Grain and garum for Caesar's army, and a chest of gold for Caesar."

Neb rolled his eyes. "Only one?"

It was three hundred leagues from Cyrene to Ruspina, plenty of time for Neb to tell his tale. "We never found them," he said. "Timur's family. I asked everywhere for the sign of the Lion of Samarkand. No one had heard of it. Or said they hadn't."

Is grunted. "We chased rumors all around Cyrenaica but nothing ever panned out." His smile was sardonic. "It's almost as if people didn't want us to find them."

"Heavens."

"He had three wives," Neb said. "I remembered him saying one of them came from north of the city and we went there first. But country folk look out for their own."

Tetisheri refilled their cups. They were sitting in the open-air cabin on the aft deck, rush mats rolled up on all four sides to admit the breeze while the canopy shaded them from the sun. The rhythmic sound of oars in and out of the water and back in again was constant. The coast of Numidia passed by on their left. Of ships, none were to be seen. The navies, too, seemed to know that things were about to come to a head.

"The silphium," Neb said heavily, "that's another story." Is emptied his cup and held it out for a refill. "But at least one with an ending."

"What about it?"

"It's gone."

"Gone?"

"It stopped growing."

Tetisheri's jaw dropped. "All by itself?"

Neb shrugged. "Depends on who you talk to. Some say the fields started thinning out and then disappeared altogether. Some say Roman merchants came with slave labor and dug up every plant they could find. Some say farmers fattened their sheep on it until there wasn't any left."

Is snorted. "Probably the sheep heard what it could do for their love lives and—" He caught Tetisheri's eye and subsided.

Neb, ignoring him, looked up at the sky. "Some say the gods have been stingy with the rain, and that silphium will return when it comes back." He sighed. "But right now, there is none to be had for love nor money."

"And even if there is," Is said, "no one is saying where, because they're keeping it for their own consumption. Can't say I blame them."

Tetisheri leaned back. "Asafetida it is then."

Everyone made a face.

Truth was, thinking about the extinction of silphium, insofar as it pertained to Sea to Sea Imports, was better than thinking about the extinction of an entire army that lay in the immediate future.

"Does anyone think Scipio has a chance? Even though he still has Caesar outnumbered?"

Silence.

Tetisheri sighed. "Good thing I brought more medical supplies for Keren's clinic, then."

But when they reached Ruspina Vitruvius was waiting with a stack of disassembled ballistae and a large collection of spearheads.

"I feel like a cabria," Tetisheri said as the sail came down, the oarsmen upped oars and they warped neatly into the slip.

Is raised an eyebrow. "A cabrio has only one horse to support. You're feeding an army. Helping to, anyway."

True enough. She raised her voice so that Vitruvius could hear her. "You'll have to wait for us to unload before we can get that lot on board."

He shook his head. "No time, and we'll need that cargo at Thapsus."

"Thapsus?" It was a small city north of Ruspina. "I thought Thapsus held for the Pompeiians."

"It did and we were besieging it when Scipio came up behind to box us in." He smiled.

"From your expression that isn't as bad as it sounds."

"We built a fort across the obvious route in, so that we have the siege works and the city at our back. There's a marsh on our left and the sea on our right." He saw their expressions and laughed. "Relax. The city surrendered to Caesar last night."

"Good to know," Is said. "At least they won't sink the ship out from under us when we try to dock."

"Keren?"

Vitruvius looked puzzled for a moment and then his face cleared. "The doctor? She was moved to Thapsus this morning. I was on my way when I saw you coming. Quicker by sea than by land." He motioned to his men. "Load it up."

"As my niece said, the hold is full," Neb said.

"Lash it to the deck then. Thapsus is only five leagues up the coast and the weather continues fair.

Tetisheri looked at Neb, who looked at Jerome, who did the captain's ritual of squinting at the sky, the clouds, the coast, the water. "Shouldn't be a problem."

"Do you even know where Thapsus is?"

He gave Neb an old-fashioned look. "I was born in Carthage, sir, and apprenticed to sea when I was eight. I could find my way to it blindfolded."

"Very well. Get this cargo loaded and let's be on our way."

16

The *Hapi II*, riding low in the water beneath its double cargo, made port just after dawn. The drums of war rolled out over the water as they approached the harbor. Vitruvius swore beneath his breath and barely waited for the first line to be made fast before he vaulted over the rail and hit the slip running. He vanished up the gangway only to reappear moments later with half a dozen legionnaires trotting at his heels. The ballistae and the spearheads were unloaded and carried off at the double.

"What about the rest of the cargo?" Neb said.

Vitruvius shook his head. "We'll worry about that after the battle."

Neb looked at Tetisheri. Tetisheri looked at Is. Is looked at Dub, who looked to the heavens for help and found none. "Let's go see what we can see? Sure, why not, what could go wrong."

The streets of the city were deserted for the most part, although Tetisheri did see one vendor with a cart full of dolmas for sale and a line of civilians and even a few legionnaires in front of it.

"The ramparts," Dub said, and led the way.

Tetisheri wanted to find Keren, but she knew the doctor would place herself as near to the action as possible and would be up to her eyebrows in blood and gore. She followed.

Many citizens of Thapsus were there on the walls before them, but not so many that everyone didn't have a clear view of the battlefield.

As the morning progressed, Tetisheri began to wish it were otherwise.

Caesar's legions faced Scipio's, from this vantage point both sides looking very similarly arrayed. The difference was Juba's elephants deployed to the right and left forward of Scipio's troops. They loomed very large compared to the soldiers in both directions, and they looked very well armored.

"*Acies triplex*," Dub said.

"What?"

"Triple line." He indicated the formations, both of which were lined up in three distinct groups. "Standard tactics, both of them."

"I thought Scipio had more men."

"So did I," Is said grimly. He nodded at the standards flying from Caesar's cohorts. "And those are veterans, not fish."

"And they're eager."

They could see a tent pitched in back of the Pompeiian forces, a banner on a pole in front of it. "Scipio," Is said, and spat.

Caesar was riding back and forth in front of his troops, speaking to them, too far for those on the city ramparts to hear anything but a few words here and there. His men were pressing forward in a single, seething body. The eagerness to be at the enemy was palpable. Tetisheri found herself leaning forward, pressing her feet against the surface of the wall, as if she, too, were in the vanguard, ready to attack.

"He's trying to hold them," Is said.

"They won't be held. They want to get this done and go home."

Dub's words reminded Tetisheri of Vitruvius. She strained to see him but there were so many, it was impossible to distinguish any one soldier.

Caesar galloped up and down again before his front line, haranguing his men. It was obvious that they weren't listening, that they didn't want to. A trumpeter somewhere in the ranks let loose with a clear, insistent call, instantly mimicked by trumpeters from all the other cohorts.

Caesar shouted something and this time, even over the din of the trumpets, they heard him clearly. "*Felicitas!*"

And then he turned and charged straight at the enemy's ranks.

In an instant the sky was filled with arrows and spears. Some struck the elephants on the right and they panicked and turned to stampede into their own troops. Men and elephants both screamed. Almost instantly Scipio's line began to fall apart. The ranks in the back were the first to break and run, but it was far too late, and they had nowhere to run to. The elephants trumpeted and stampeded, trampling anyone and anything that came within their path. They crashed through ballistae and siege engines, leaving nothing behind but splinters and flattened soldiers who couldn't run fast enough to escape them.

Caesar's legions fell on them with no mercy, although without Caesar, as he had retired to the rear, where he nearly fell from his horse into the arms of his aides.

Near them on the wall a citizen of Thapsus cheered, and was as quickly hushed by his fellows.

"One of his fits," Is said, and Dub nodded.

"Fits?" Neb said.

"He has the falling sickness," Dub said.

"Caesar?" Neb said in disbelief.

Dub nodded, eyes fixed on the battle. Neither he nor Is looked in the least concerned that Caesar was subject to a disease that had him falling off his horse in the middle of a battle. Certainly his troops took no notice and continued to charge forward.

Neb and Tetisheri exchanged a nervous glance and remained where they were. Minutes later, much to their relief, Caesar remounted his horse and charged back into the fray, sword out and soon bloodied.

There were heartfelt groans from the Thapsuns on the wall, though.

After that, it was simple butchery on a massive scale.

Tetisheri watched with a numbed, distant horror as Scipio's troops cast aside their weapons, only to be struck down in the act of surrendering. The Roman legions moved inexorably forward, hacking and hewing and cutting. The battlefield was strewn with severed limbs and heads and entrails, turning into a vile soup of creeping red. The acrid, sickening smell of spilled blood drifted toward those on the wall and over it to invade the city. The screams of pleading, dying men in their thousands vied with the harsh caws of crows and gulls and hawks flapping over the wounded and the dead, waiting their chance to feed. The Roman troops killed the elephants, too, where they could, a task that became easier as they brought up their ballistae to target Scipio's fleeing troops. Only those few who fled the fight early escaped.

The Battle of Thapsus was won before noon, but the killing went on until nightfall.

17

Tetisheri stirred from her paralysis finally and opened stiff lips to speak in a voice not her own. "I want to find Keren."

"She'll be there." Is pointed at a large, square tent pitched near the gates of the city. Men were already being carried there on stretchers.

She was glad to turn her back on the horror before the city's walls. She followed Is down to the main gate, both doors of which stood whole and open. The city's surrender might have saved their infrastructure, but Caesar would make them pay for their previous intransigence. By the glum expressions on the citizens' faces they knew that full well and only waited to discover how much.

The tent was full of cots, perhaps a hundred of them, holding men in various states of disrepair. It was mostly wounds from blades and arrows and none of them seemed all that serious, given the carnage on the battlefield outside.

They were all Roman soldiers here. The winning side of this battle was not going to suffer many casualties, and none of Caesar's medical resources were going to be wasted on the enemy. Should any of them survive.

Keren, her tunic stained with blood from shoulder to hem, leaned over a man who had been placed on a cot in the back. Tetisheri threaded her way through the wounded, none of whom were hurt enough not to eye her appreciatively and offer comments and invitations. That is until they came under Is and Dub and Uncle Neb's eyes. Crixus nodded at them from beyond Keren. "Did you see?"

"We watched from the walls."

Crixus's expression was somber and subdued, unnatural for him. "That wasn't a battle, that was an extermination."

Dub nodded. "No argument here." He looked down at Keren's patient. "What happened to him?"

"Crushed by one of Juba's elephants, looks like," Crix spat to one side. "I hate those things."

"Don't worry. Caesar is slaughtering them all as we speak."

"Good."

"Pastor!" Is elbowed Dub out of the way and stood staring down at the man on the cot, his face white and shocked.

Pastor looked all right, Tetisheri thought, momentarily puzzled, and then her gaze traveled down past his chest and her breath caught in her throat. His legs had been literally flattened between hips and knees, as if they had been crushed with a hammer the size of which only Heracles could have raised.

Or the large, flat foot of a beast. Say, an elephant.

His head down to his belly looked normal, his knees to his feet the same. But belly to knee there was nothing remaining of him that was recognizably human. Cartilage had broken or been severed and stood up here and there like ends of gristle in a tough cut of meat. Slivers of bone gleamed whitely through a mash of flesh and cloth. A slippery coil of entrails that had somehow escaped ruin steamed slightly in the cooling air of the afternoon. The cot was red with blood. More of it dripped steadily to the floor. The smells of blood and piss and shit clogged her throat.

It took several moments before Tetisheri could convince herself that this was the same man she had last seen standing in the doorway of the Waterfront Inn in Cyrene, large, confident, carrying the news that had led him and all of them inevitably to this place, on this day.

She couldn't conceive how they had kept him in one piece long enough to bring him to Keren.

The light seemed to dim, and then she felt Dub's hand slide beneath her elbow. "Steady on, girl. Deep breaths, in, out, one after the other. That's it."

She blinked and breathed and the scene came back into focus. In another moment her nose accustomed itself to the smells and the wave of nausea subsided.

Tetisheri had seen people die before. She'd even seen them die in war. This—this was even more obscene. The man on the cot, a third of him gone, stamped out of substance, of volume, of presence, of being a part of a greater whole.

A thread of a voice issued up from what was surely soon

to be a corpse. "Isidorus? Is that you?" Brown eyes opened and looked up.

Neb said, "That's the soldier who brought the news of Caesar's landing to my reception." He sounded as if he didn't believe it himself.

"One of Scipio's?" Dub looked over her shoulder. "How did he end up in here?"

Is looked at Keren, who shook her head. She didn't have to say anything.

"Move me outside." Pastor looked only at Is. "Let me die with the sun on my face."

Is looked again at Keren, who lifted her shoulders in a slight shrug as if to say Pastor would die wherever he was. Or perhaps that she was fine with him being moved so that she could use the space for someone who might survive. Perhaps both those things.

They picked him up, the four of them, Neb and Tetisheri and Dub and Is, cot and all, and carried him out of the tent to a quiet spot in a copse of acacia trees located outside the line of battle. Is knelt down on one knee. "Better?"

"Yes. Thanks." Pastor blinked and his voice sounded a little stronger. "Is? Isidorus?"

"Yes, it's me."

Pastor looked as if he might move his hand but couldn't manage it. Is took it in his own. It was the left one, whose arm bore the scar he had received at Bibracte. What might have been a smile pulled at the dead man's lips. "Did you fight with us?"

"No."

"Good. At least one of us had that much sense." He

laughed, or tried to, and coughed blood. "Ah gods," he said, staring at the sky. "Fucking elephants."

"How did you get here?" Dub said. "These are Caesar's men."

"Someone mistook me for one of his. That woman doctor, I think she knows, but she was kind. She gave me something for the pain. Not that I can feel much." He looked at Is again. "I'm glad to have a friend to see me off at the end." He didn't seem to notice the rest of them gathered around, listening.

"Tell us about Timur." Tetisheri kept her voice neutral, no accusation, just a simple request for information.

"Who? Timur?"

"The factor in Cyrene," Is said, his voice equally steady. "You were seen where his body was found."

Pastor's eyes came back into focus. "I knew you were more than a mere guard. Spy? Who for?" Is said nothing. "Agent then. Ah. Alexandria. Cleopatra? Is she as beautiful as they say?"

Is's shoulders raised in a slight shrug. "It's hard to see past her brains."

A shudder ran over Pastor's body, and Tetisheri realized he was laughing, or trying to. "A smart woman in a tight stola. No wonder old Pontifex fell so hard."

"Timur," Is said again.

"Timur. Him. Yes. He died too quickly to tell us where he'd hidden it."

"Hidden what?"

Pastor's eyes wandered past Is's face to the sky. "So blue. So beautiful."

"Was it a ledger you were looking for?" Tetisheri said. "A business ledger, perhaps?"

Pastor, watching the sky as his last moments passed, didn't hear her. Or didn't want to.

"You were in business together." Tetisheri kept her voice gentle but insistent. "You needed an agent, Pastor, didn't you? A registered agent for the slave auction."

She couldn't see Is's face but his shoulders were hunched over Pastor, as if to protect the man on the cot from her relentless voice.

"A registered agent is how the city takes its piece." She looked at Uncle Neb and saw the slow dawn of understanding, and of grief.

"It's a large upfront fee plus an annual cut of the earnings," he said.

"And there was no way you could afford that big a fee when you were just starting out, was there, Pastor?" Tetisheri said. "Timur couldn't afford one himself. Few can."

Pastor said nothing for long enough for all of them to think he would never speak again.

"Then who bought it for him?" But Dub was looking at Neb, too, and he already knew the answer.

"I did." The pearl at the end of Uncle Neb's beard hung limp and lusterless. "It was a long time ago, when I was expanding my routes. I needed a factor in Cyrene. I'd done business with Timur before." He raised a shoulder and let it fall. "He seemed to me a good man."

The man on the cot came back to life.

"We'd been working together for over a decade." Pastor coughed again. Another gush of blood stained his tunic and the air wheezed out of him and back in again. The state his body was in, it was amazing he could still breathe at all, let alone speak. "It's not like we ever got paid, by Caesar, or Scipio. They always made big promises to make us fight but they never kept them." He looked at Is. "You know."

"I know." Is's voice was steady.

"One of the men in my squad had been a sailor, with enough experience so we didn't get lost. We had a small ship. Wasn't much to look at, but it floated. Once or twice a year we'd take the ship and raid some little village, usually Greek, too small to have protection, and sail back to Cyrene and sell them. That was where Timur came in."

"And Cotta?" Tetisheri's question came out in a harder tone than she'd meant it to. Is cast her an angry glance over his shoulder.

"So blue. What makes it so blue?" Pastor was wandering again, or maybe found it convenient to wander when a question concerning Julius Caesar's favorite cousin and most trusted advisor was put to him.

"They would need someone high up to keep them out of trouble with the navy at sea and Juba and the prefect there," Tetisheri said.

Another silence, but Pastor spoke again, eyes still fixed on the sky. "He was happy to help, for a cut." He coughed again, wheezed again. There was less blood this time and his skin was graying. "For a while, for years even, it was a sweet deal. We made enough money to invest in other businesses."

"The tavern," Is said.

"The boarding house," Dub said.

"And other things, but the slave business was what kept

everything else going. And then the little bastard started skimming."

Pastor tried to turn his head to spit and couldn't. The saliva dribbled down his chin. Is wiped it away with the neck of Pastor's tunic.

Anger over the betrayal lent the dying man a burst of strength. "Like he wasn't making enough money on the deal already. A few of us followed him home one night and confronted him. He knew we were coming—I still think that asshole Rufus gave us away, Timur probably bribed him—and he got his family out before we could use them to work on him. So we had to work on him instead. He died too quickly, though. Heart gave out, I guess. And we never found that fucking ledger. It would have told us how much he stole and maybe if we could get it back, and how."

Tetisheri felt Neb's gaze on her and looked up to meet his eyes. She gave a faint nod. He hadn't been far off on the motive. It wasn't money, but it was where they thought they could find it.

"How did you know there was a ledger?"

"He carried it with him everywhere, didn't he?" Pastor gasped for the air his chest was becoming incapable of drawing in. "I went back more than once, looking for it. Never found it."

"And Fulvio?"

"Cotta saw that we were short. He sent Fulvio to find out why. I spotted him watching us. And then I pulled a bait and switch and followed him to Timur's house."

"How did he know where it was?"

"That prick Rufus again, probably." Pastor coughed again, more weakly this time.

"Why did you kill Fulvio?" Neb asked.

Pastor found enough energy to glare. "He didn't give me much of a choice, did he? He wasn't happy when he found Timur and he didn't want to waste time listening to explanations. Him or me. I preferred me." He blinked at the sky. "Not that it matters now." He looked at Is. "Thanks. For being here."

"You're welcome. Thanks for the hospitality."

"You were good company."

"And you."

The two men grinned at each other, and then Pastor coughed again, more violently, his head half raised. This time the gush of blood overflowed the edge of the cot. When it stopped, his head had fallen back and Pastor was staring unblinkingly at the blue sky, the tension ebbing from what was left of his body as the light left his eyes.

Is closed them with a gentle hand, and bent his head.

Nebenteru had walked some distance away. Tetisheri followed. They stood with their backs to the site of the battle, their faces to the sea, and to where home lay waiting.

"So this is the end of our first, glorious shakedown cruise," he said glumly. "First, our factor was murdered, and now his entirely unrepentant killer has gone beyond our reach. Then we went looking for silphium, and found none."

"Because none was to be found, Uncle."

He sighed. "Timur—I'm sorry he went that way. Painful. Horrible."

"I'm not." He looked at her, momentarily startled out of his gloom. "If he cheated them, Uncle, he cheated us. You've said it yourself. Thieves never stop at one theft, once they learn how." She shook her head. "No. He earned that death."

He narrowed his eyes. "You've been spending too much time with Cleopatra."

He wasn't joking, but she couldn't help but laugh a little.

"You didn't see his body, Tetisheri. They weren't—gentle."

"No. I don't expect they were."

Then she saw that his pearl was drooping again, so she put her arm around him and gave him the only comfort she could think of. "When does Demetrius say the *Hapi III* will be ready to launch?"

EPÍLOGOS

MAY, 46 BCE
SIWA OASIS

Tetisheri narrowed her eyes against the glare. "Is that—that looks like the *Nut*."

Three weeks they had been at Thapsus following the battle, as Keren would not leave until the last of her patients had died or been discharged, and Tetisheri refused to leave without her.

There was less work for Keren than anyone might have guessed. At the Battle of Thapsus Caesar's legions had suffered perhaps fifty casualties.

Scipio and Juba lost ten thousand. It was a difficult number for any of them to assimilate, even the veterans. The killing ground had been rendered into a crematorium of bodies and body parts piled high. Mercifully, the onshore breeze blew the smell and the ash inland.

The harbor was full of supply barges and troop ships, so they watched the small ship slip nimbly between them, up oars at the last possible minute, and with a muted sound of wood grating over gravel slide gently bow first onto the beach. A dark, burly man with close-clipped hair and beard made his way forward and vaulted onto the shore, not even getting his feet wet. He straightened his tunic and marched up the incline to stop before her. He bowed. "Lady."

"Captain."

"Markos, lady."

"Tetisheri, Markos."

His teeth were a gleam of white against his beard. "Your business here is complete?"

"It is."

"Good. You are needed elsewhere."

"You have orders for me?"

"No." He nodded at the *Nut*. "But he does."

She followed his gesture and saw someone standing in the stern, at first only an outline against the sun. As her vision adjusted she saw that he was tall, fair of hair, green of eye, had a military set to his shoulders and an ever-present gladius at his hip. Wearing Cleopatra's livery now.

Without thinking she took a step forward.

When she saw him smile, she began to run. He jumped down to the shore and caught her, grinning, and bent his head to kiss her soundly.

"I can't believe it!" She was half laughing, half gasping for breath. "She sent you to bring me home?"

"Well…" He set her down.

She watched his grin fade. "What?"

"We're not going home." He looked over her shoulder, and she turned to see Julius Caesar coming down the gangway with Aurelius Cotta and a small, tight group of legionnaires behind him. None of the Romans looked the least bit conscious of having perpetrated a bloodbath three weeks before. Leaving a butcher's bill of ten thousand for the cities who had opposed Caesar to pay was business as usual, evidently.

No prisoners, no pardons. Vitruvius had been matter-of-fact about it and he had meant what he said. He had returned to Alexandria a week before on another freighter, there to take up his post at the Mouseion again. He did not appear haunted by Thapsus, either. What remained of the enemy had been conscripted into the *exercitus Romanus* with little fuss, and with positive enthusiasm when it came to Juba's light cavalry. Even now Caesar's new, amalgamated forces were drilling on the grounds where so much blood had been spilled.

"As if they need reminding," Is said.

"That he could have killed them all?" Dub nodded. "Caesar knows how to drive home a lesson."

Tetisheri repressed a shudder. The smells of blood and putrefaction lingered even now, days, weeks after the battle, competing with the smell of roasting flesh as the bodies were piled into small mountains and burned. Caesar punished the men of Thapsus for their disloyalty by conscripting them into the necessary labor. They dragged themselves back into the city each night with ravaged mien under the unsympathetic eyes of their legionnaire guards.

She thought she could have borne it better if Caesar and his forces had not gone about the business from start to finish so... so methodically.

The *Hapi II* with Neb and Is and Dub and Keren and Crixus aboard left for Alexandria. The *Nut* sailed at the same time, both ships with the wind at their backs. The *Nut* skimmed over the water like a low-flying bird and left the other, much larger boat far behind. Tetisheri spared a thought for Uncle Neb's feelings at watching the *Nut*'s stern recede in the distance. But only a thought. Awareness of Apollodorus at her side again took all her attention.

Caesar and his men occupied the stern. Apollodorus and Tetisheri retired to the tiny bow, where they could be at least partially hidden by the mast and the sail and where the noise of the oars splashing would mask what they said. They still took care to speak softly.

"Where were you? Every body I saw at Thapsus I was terrified would be you."

He kept his eyes on the water rushing by, on the dip and rise of the oars, on the eddies the blades left behind. "I was with Juba. We were at Thapsus." Since she could hardly bear to look away from his face she saw him close his eyes briefly. "Against all advice, they split their forces. It was their downfall. When it became obvious the day was lost Juba and Petreius escaped with most of the Numidian forces. When they stopped running, the two of them got drunk and fought a duel, with the understanding that the winner would kill himself afterward."

She must have made a sound for he glanced at her and away again. "Yes, I know. Idiotic. But I was there and I saw it, so it must be true. Petreius won, if you can call it that, and then ran himself through with his own sword."

After a moment Tetisheri said, "Better by their own hands than Caesar's, I suppose."

"They thought so." He took a deep breath and let it out slowly. "It seemed to me to be high time to leave, so I made my way to the coast and found an empty supply boat bound for Alexandria. I had enough gold for the captain to pretend I was invisible." A soundless laugh. "He probably thought I was a deserter."

He stretched. "I reported to the queen, who sent me back on the *Nut*. And here I am."

"And here we are."

He smiled at the sea. "And here we are." His voice changed. "What happened to Scipio?"

Tetisheri grimaced. "He fled the battle aboard a ship. When Caesar's fleet caught up to him he stabbed himself, but his people got to him in time. They sewed him up and when they left him to recover he woke up, ripped out the stitches, and tore out his entrails with his own hands."

"Like Cato? Gods." He sighed. "Romans are determined to die hard. And Pompey's sons?"

"Escaped." At least she wouldn't have to send word to Cornelia of Sextus's death.

They arrived at their destination in two days' sail.

"Paraetonium?" Tetisheri said. It was one of the major

grain ports of Egypt. She'd been here several times in the past months. "Why here?"

"You'll see."

They left the *Nut* with Markos at the harbor, moored next to a larger ship very familiar to Tetisheri, and mounted the horses that had been left for them. They headed south through groves of olives and date palms and fields of grain and beans, watered by artesian wells foaming up from the earth. A toll held them up but not for long, as Apollodorus had a fat purse to get them through with no questions asked. Although one of the toll keepers, a grizzled veteran of at least sixty years, snapped to attention when he saw Caesar and tossed off a salute. Caesar nodded but said nothing and they were through and back on the road.

At dusk they arrived at Siwa Oasis, where the setting sun offered relief from the heat of the day. The buildings and temples of the small town clustered around one edge of a large, elongated lake. The streets were broad and lined with trees. Fountains bubbled up on every corner, featuring statues of gods old and new. One of the newer ones was of Isis holding Horus in her arms, her face raised to Amun-Re, eyes closed. She bore a remarkable resemblance to Cleopatra. Tetisheri saw Caesar give it a long look as they went by, and had a feeling another statue would be raised before long, one in the image of Osiris but with the look of a Roman general.

They left the town behind, following the edge of the lake, passing more fields and groves. Farmers looked up from their labors to watch them pass, a break in their day before they bent back over their hoes.

Outside the city the road left the lakeside and turned

more toward the southwest. They traversed a small pass between two hills and came upon another, much smaller lake. A collection of tanned canvas tents stood on the shore, with a pavilion tent pitched apart from the rest.

A sycamore in full leaf towered over it, and through flaps tied back a laden table and a broad, cushioned bed piled high with colorful pillows could be seen inside. An Egyptian woman stood before it, young, dark hair unbound, no jewelry, clad only in a simple white sheath. Two attendants busied themselves untying the canvas sides of the pavilion and fastening them together to enclose a whole, after which they left to go to their tent, pitched what had probably been carefully calculated to be just out of earshot. A company of Egyptian soldiers was picketed around the rim of the little valley that enclosed the lake.

The nearest soldier was Hesperos, whom Tetisheri had last seen at the door of the palace. They nodded to each other.

Caesar, who had said almost nothing the entire journey, spoke. "Get some rest, men. Those tents over there are yours and if I know our hostess there will be food and wine aplenty. You, too, Orry."

Orry? Tetisheri mouthed at Apollodorus, who grinned.

Caesar kicked his horse into a canter. When he reached the pavilion he swung down and took two strides forward to snatch Cleopatra up into his arms. Her laughter echoed across the water. They disappeared into the pavilion.

"Come on, men," Cotta said. "We'll be getting more sleep than Caesar does this night."

As they rode off Tetisheri looked at Apollodorus. "Alone at last."

He smiled at her and she shivered at the look in his eyes. "Come with me."

"Anywhere."

Ten minutes later they topped a small rise. Below them, a pool was cupped in a tiny vale of golden sand. The water gleamed a rich, deep blue even in the dim light of evening. A small tent had been pitched next to it. Apollodorus led the way down the slope and they dismounted. He nodded. "Go ahead, take a look. Charmion and Iras promised they'd provide the necessaries."

She left him untacking the horses and went to explore.

The tent was luxuriously furnished with a bed heaped high with cushions, piled on top of a fine linen coverlet. A fire had been laid before the tent flap. It lit at the first spark. There was a food bundle with dishes and utensils and a small metal pot.

She walked down to the edge of the pond. The moon had risen, Nut shining down on the tiny vale so strongly that she could see through the water to the smooth rocks lining the bottom. She stripped to the skin and walked in up to her waist. It was still warm from the day's sun. The pond looked long enough for ten overhand strokes and she lost no time in proving it so. When she tired of swimming she floated on her back and watched the stars emerge one by one in the steadily darkening sky. They looked more familiar and somehow more friendly after all the nights she had spent watching them move overhead during the past months.

Wavelets washed over her body and she turned her head to see Apollodorus standing at the edge of the water. He kicked off his sandals and pulled his tunic over his head, leaving his clothes in the sand next to hers. He waded into the water and reached out a hand to pull her to him. She let her feet drift down to the rocks and stood, so close she could feel his breath on her cheek.

When he spoke his voice was hoarse. "Tetisheri, forgive me. It has been too long. I don't think I can go slowly."

"Then don't." She slid her hand into his hair and pulled his head down to hers.

It wasn't slow, and it wasn't gentle, either. Tetisheri was sure he'd left bruises, but then she'd left scratches. They came together once in the water, again in the sand when they become more interested in each other than in dinner, and a third time in the early hours of the morning when she woke and found him next to her. She came up on her knees and touched him until he woke everywhere and then she took him as he had taken her, hard and fast, culminating in an explosion of bliss that threatened to melt her spine.

She fell forward, gasping for breath, hearing his heart thunder in her ear.

Outside, the birds began to stir. They lay together, content, and watched the world fill with light. After a while they went down to the pool and took exquisite care in washing each other's bodies. Enough of that and she climbed him the way she had in Laurus' house, to take him inside her, rising and falling faster and faster until they both shouted their pleasure to the sky.

Later she said, "Why here?"

"Well." Apollodorus's lips quirked up in a smile. "Alexander himself came here to consult the oracle."

"Of course." The sun felt warm and caressing on her skin. They hadn't bothered to dress. "And the oracle told him he would rule the world. Where Alexander sought and received validation, so would Caesar. And she would know that. I expect they'll ride over to the oracle in a day or two." She turned her head and found him propped up on his elbow, looking at her. "Did she bring the boy?"

He flopped back on the sand. "Did you think she wouldn't?"

"I suppose not. He's Caesar's only son, and this isn't like Alexandria, or Rome, where holding the child would look like he was acknowledging him. Here he can enjoy holding his only son without the Senate and people of Rome fearing he's going to put an Egyptian woman on the throne next to him." A bird chirped, and another answered it. "How long do we get to stay here, did she say?"

"No." With a gentle forefinger, as if to memorize it, he traced the line of her profile, forehead, nose, lips, chin, throat.

Her eyes closed beneath his touch. "Is she going to Rome with him?"

"I should be asking you that."

She thought about it, frowning a little. "Not yet," she said finally. "I don't think she wants to be present when Arsinoë is forced to march in Caesar's triumph, and especially not when Arsinoë is strangled."

"Not from affection, surely."

She smiled a little. "No. But it's possible the Roman mob would want her to show mercy, one sister to another."

"The very last thing she wants to do."

"Indeed not." She watched a songbird skim over the surface of the water and swoop up to land in the fronds of a date palm, there to give joyous voice to the day. She knew how he felt. "She won't leave the city for long anyway. The birth of Caesarion helped but Alexandrians are notoriously fickle. The Greeks especially are still angry at her for allowing so many Egyptians into the city."

"Half the Palace Guard is Egyptian."

"Exactly. The Greeks are feeling outnumbered. It makes them nervous." She sighed. "And Caesar still has to settle with the last of the Pompeiians."

"Gnaeus and Sextus."

"Yes. Caesar won't be satisfied until any threat of a Pompeiian rebellion is utterly extinguished."

His chest rose and fell in a sigh. "So the war isn't over."

"No, and she's not about to go to Rome if Caesar is off fighting somewhere else."

"She's not beloved in Rome."

"No, she is not."

Enough. The great ones would be pulling their strings again soon enough, involving them in their machinations, manipulating their actions, usurping their lives.

But not today.

She rolled into the water and splashed him hard and dived before he could retaliate. He caught her ankle easily and brought her back to the surface. She smoothed her hands over his head, sluicing the water from his face, and smiled into his green eyes.

"There is no war here."

And there wasn't. There was only love.

ACKNOWLEDGMENTS

Tetisheri's notes on silphium are taken from the 2019 Delphi Classics Kindle edition of *The Collected Works of Theophrastus*. More recently, *National Geographic* wrote a lengthy article about it. I went with Theophrastus's spelling as he has the seniority.

The story of Tebtynis (the Roman absentee landlord) comes from *Life in Egypt under Roman Rule* and *Greeks in Ptolemaic Egypt*, both written by Naphtali Lewis and published by the American Society of Papyrologists. The text consists of translations of papyri and are hands down the best contemporary source material for life as it was lived then that I've yet found for the Eye of Isis novels. A huge tip of the hat to *Lapham's Quarterly*, too, who first alerted me to their existence.

My version of the Battle of Thapsus was informed largely but not entirely by Adrian Goldsworthy's account in *Caesar*. More details on the care and feeding of Roman legions came from Stephen Dando-Collins' *Legions of Rome*, Guy de la Bédoyère's *Gladius*, and Philip Matyszak's *Legionary*.

Caesar's supply chain issues prior to Thapsus were real

and acute. Caesar was always broke, and it was no stretch at all to imagine that his closest advisor would turn to the most lucrative business in the classical world, the slave trade, to help top up the operating expenses. All empires are built on slavery. Rome was no different. It was an easy fictional segue to the *Hapi II* being conscripted into supplying his army, and certainly my fictional Cotta has never made any secret that Caesar's priorities took precedence with him.

The Tenth Legion was Caesar's favorite, true, or it was until they refused service outside the walls of Rome until Caesar paid them what he promised (see above). When they joined him in Africa, as punishment he made them fight where they would suffer the most casualties.

Juba was conscripting everything with a pulse in advance of Caesar's invasion. All the able-bodied men who didn't move fast enough were put forcibly under arms. Caesar was vastly outnumbered in this campaign but he was by far the better general and he was lucky that Bocchus hated Juba as much as Juba hated Caesar. I never found any mention as to why Bocchus hated Juba (it could be as simple as raids over a common border), but in Juba's case his hatred was well-founded: Caesar really did pull his beard and sleep with his wife. (I put those two in the order in which I believe Juba would have ranked them in importance.)

Juba had an estimated 120 war elephants, true. They panicked and stampeded back over their own lines at Thapsus, also true. Soldiers on any side hated elephants equally because they were never sure going into battle which way the elephants would charge. The Battle of Thapsus is generally held to be the last in which war elephants were deployed.

Cyrene, Cyrenaica. I defy you to find any two contemporaneous maps that use those same names twice for the same place, or in the same location, for that matter. I colluded with Dr. Cherie Northon, my mapmaker, and decided to simplify things: Cyrene would be the city, Cyrenaica the province. I did find one reference to Apollonia, defined as the community around the harbor, and decided to meld the two under a single name, Cyrene, to save confusion, mine and the reader's.

Cartographers then also took a large-minded view of the locations of Mauretania, Numidia, and Cyrenaica, swapping them back and forth with gay abandon. The map at the beginning of the book is my and Cherie's best guess at what a map of North Africa might have looked like at that time. I love fiction.

ABOUT THE AUTHOR

DANA STABENOW was born in Anchorage, Alaska and raised on a 75-foot fishing tender. She knew there was a warmer, drier job out there somewhere and found it in writing. Her first book in the bestselling Kate Shugak series, *A Cold Day for Murder*, received an Edgar Award from the Mystery Writers of America. *Abduction of a Slave* is her fourth mystery set in Ancient Egypt.

Contact Dana via her website:
www.stabenow.com

WELCOME TO CLEOPATRA'S EGYPT

a place of labyrinthine mysteries
and deadly intrigues

in the **EYE OF ISIS** series by

DANA STABENOW